FATHER AND SON

FATHER AND SON

BJØRNSTJERNE BJØRNSON

Translated with an introduction
by Augusta Plesner and Susan Rugeley-Powers

Cockatrice Books
Y diawl a'm llaw chwith

Arne: A Sketch of Norwegian Life, translated by Augusta Plesner and Susan Rugeley-Powers, was first published by Sever, Francis & Co., Boston in 1869. It was republished in 2020 by Cockatrice Books with a new title and minor editorial changes.

This edition copyright © Cockatrice Books 2022
www.cockatrice-books.com
mail@cockatrice-books.com

Published as part of the Cymru'r Byd series, celebrating the literature of Wales and the world.

CONTENTS

Translator's Preface   7

I. How the Cliff was Clad   13

II. A Cloudy Dawn   17

III. Seeing an Old Love   31

IV. The Unlamented Death   44

V. 'He Had in His Mind a Song.'   55

VI. Strange Tales   64

VII. The Soliloquy in the Barn   74

VIII. The Shadows on the Water   81

IX. The Nutting-Party   92

X. Loosening the Weather-Vane   112

XI. Eli's Sickness   128

XII. A Glimpse of Spring   139

XIII. Margit Consults the Clergyman   149

XIV. Finding a Lost Song   162

XV. Somebody's Future Home   174

XVI. The Double Wedding   195

Notes   200

TRANSLATOR'S PREFACE

The story which is here first presented in an English form, is one of Herr Bjørnson's best works. In the original, it has already attained a very wide circulation throughout Northern Europe, and is there generally recognized as one of the truest and most beautiful representations of Norwegian life. At the present time, when there is among us a constantly increasing interest in all things pertaining to the Scandinavian nations, this work possesses great claims to attention, not only through its intrinsic merits, but also from the fact that it is one of the very few works which can, in the fullest sense, be termed Norwegian. During the long political union of Norway with Denmark, Norwegian literature was so deeply imbued by Danish thought and feeling, that it could not be considered national. After those political changes in 1814, which placed Norway among the free nations, she strove to take an independent position; and she produced several gifted writers who endeavoured to create a national literature; but she had for many years no great works unimpressed with the old Danish stamp. Not till 1857, when a young and comparatively unknown writer published a book called *Synnove Solbakken*, can the distinct literary life of Norway be considered to have commenced. That young writer was Bjørnstjerne Bjørnson. Since the appearance of *Synnove Solbakken,* he has produced the present story, a few other short sketches, and several dramatic works. All these productions are, both in subject and style, thoroughly representative of the grand old nation whence they sprang; and they are, moreover, so full of original poetic beauty and descriptive power, that they have stamped their author as one of the greatest writers in Northern Europe.

While presenting this work from one who so well deserves to be known and honoured by all, we very much wish we could also present a sketch of his history. But, so far as we have been able to ascertain, there is very little material; for, happily, Herr Bjørnson is yet young, and in the midst of his literary career; and therefore only a small part of his life-story can yet be told. We have, however, obtained a few interesting details, principally from a little sketch in the Danish of Herr Clemens Petersen.

Herr Bjørnson is the son of a clergyman; and was born in 1832, at Kvikne, a lonely parish on the Dovre Fjeld. In his earliest years, he was so far from being marked by any unusual degree of mental development, that he was even regarded as 'stupid': he seems to have been at that time merely a strong-limbed, happy, playful little fellow. Whenever he was at home, he constantly made the quiet parsonage a scene of confusion and uproar through his wild play. 'Things,' says Herr Petersen, 'which had within the memory of man never been moved, were flung down; chairs and tables spun round; and all the girls and boys in the place ran about with him in noisy play; while his mother used to clasp her hands in fright, and declare he must soon be sent off to sea.' When, in his twelfth year, he went to school, he appears to have been just as little characterized by any unusual mental development, and just as much by physical activity. He was placed on the lowest form to learn with the little boys. But when he got out-doors into the playground, he was at once among the leaders, and feared nobody: on one occasion he soundly thrashed the strongest boy in the whole school. Although, however, no one else at this time saw any promise of his future greatness, he had himself a presentiment of it: deep in the heart of the rough Norwegian school-boy, who seemed to think of little but play, was hidden a purpose to become an author, and even the greatest of all authors.

At the University, Herr Bjørnson was as little distinguished by intellectual attainments as at school; and he never passed the second part of his examination. He seems, indeed, never to have been a very earnest student of any writings save those 'manuscripts of God' contained in the great volumes of Nature and human society. These, few have studied more earnestly, or translated with greater force and beauty.

While studying at the University, Herr Bjørnson's literary purposes still remained; and during this time he produced his first drama, *Valburg*, though he had then never read one dramatic work through, or been at a theatre more than twice in his life. He sent *Valburg* to the managers of the theatre at Christiania; and it was accepted. But as soon as he had been to the theatre a few times, he decided that, in its present state, it was not a fit medium for the expression of his inner life; and he therefore took his piece back before it had been played. For a while afterwards, he devoted a great part of his time to dramatic criticism. He attacked some of the prevalent errors in theatrical affairs with so much force and boldness that he greatly exasperated the orthodox actors and managers, and thus brought down much annoyance upon himself. His criticisms were, however, the means of greatly improving the Norwegian drama, especially by partly releasing it from the undue Danish influence which prevented it from becoming truly national.

Herr Bjørnson subsequently abandoned his dramatic criticism, left Christiania, and returned to his father's home in the country. Here he assiduously devoted himself to literary work, but without very satisfactory tangible results. Next, he went back to Christiania, and employed himself in writing for various periodicals, where he inserted a series of short sketches which, although far inferior to his subsequent and more mature productions, bore strong indications of genius, and attracted much attention. But, meanwhile, their noble young author lived a sad and weary life — depressed by the fear that his best hopes would never be realized — harassed by pecuniary difficulties, and tormented by the most cruel persecution. Next, he went to Uppsala, where he still employed himself upon periodical literature, and had an interval of comparative quiet and happiness. Thence, he travelled to Hamburg, and afterwards to Copenhagen. Here he remained half a year, living a quiet, studious life, and associating with some of the most eminent men in the city. 'Those days,' said he, 'were the best I ever had.' Certainly, they were very fruitful ones. In them he produced one complete work, parts of several others, and the first half of *Synnove Solbakken*, the tale which was destined to place him in the foremost rank of Scandinavian writers. It is a remarkable fact that shortly before he left Copenhagen with all this heap of wealth, he had passed through a crisis of such miserable depression that he was just about to abandon literary labour for ever, through a sense of utter unfitness to perform it.

From Copenhagen, Herr Bjørnson returned to Norway, and was for two years manager of the theatre at Bergen, occupying most of the time in the training of actors. Thence he went, with his young wife, again to Christiania, where he for some months edited *Aftenbladet*, one of the leading Norwegian journals.

Relative to Herr Bjørnson's subsequent life and labours, there is but very little available information.

Of our own part in the following pages, we have but to say we have earnestly endeavoured to deal faithfully and reverently with Herr Bjørnson's work, and to render nearly every passage as fully and literally as the construction of the two languages permits. The only exceptions are two very short, and comparatively very unimportant passages, which we have ventured to omit, because we believed they would render the book less acceptable to English readers.

London, June, 1866.

I.

HOW THE CLIFF WAS CLAD

Between two cliffs lay a deep ravine, with a full stream rolling heavily through it over boulders and rough ground. It was high and steep, and one side was bare, save at the foot, where clustered a thick, fresh wood, so close to the stream that the mist from the water lay upon the foliage in spring and autumn. The trees stood looking upwards and forwards, unable to move either way.

'What if we were to clothe the Cliff?' said the Juniper one day to the foreign Oak that stood next him. The Oak looked down to find out who was speaking, and then looked up again without answering a word. The Stream worked so hard that it grew white; the North wind rushed through the ravine, and shrieked in the fissures; and the bare Cliff hung heavily over and felt cold. 'What if we were to clothe the Cliff?' said the Juniper to the Fir on the other side. 'Well, if anybody is to do it, I suppose we must,' replied the Fir, stroking his beard; 'what dost thou think?' he added, looking over to the Birch. 'In God's name, let us clothe it,' answered the Birch, glancing timidly towards the Cliff, which hung over her so heavily that she felt as if she could scarcely breathe. And thus, although they were but three, they agreed to clothe the Cliff. The Juniper went first.

When they had gone a little way they met the Heather. The Juniper seemed as though he meant to pass her by. 'Nay, let us take the Heather with us,' said the Fir. So on went the Heather. Soon the Juniper began to slip. 'Lay hold on me,' said the Heather. The Juniper did so, and where there was only a little crevice the Heather put in one finger, and where she had got in one finger the Juniper put in his whole hand. They crawled and climbed, the Fir heavily behind with the Birch. 'It is a work of charity,' said the Birch.

But the Cliff began to ponder what little things these could be that came clambering up it. And when it had thought over this a few hundred years, it sent down a little Brook to see about it. It was just spring flood, and the Brook rushed on till she met the Heather. 'Dear, dear Heather, canst thou not let me pass? I am so little,' said the Brook. The Heather, being very busy, only raised herself a little, and worked on. The Brook slipped under her, and ran onwards. 'Dear, dear Juniper, canst thou not let me pass? I am so little,' said the Brook. The Juniper glanced sharply at her; but as the Heather had let her pass, he thought he might do so as well. The Brook slipped under him, and ran on till she came where the Fir stood panting on a crag. 'Dear, dear Fir, canst thou not let me pass? I am so little,' the Brook said, fondly kissing the Fir on his foot. The Fir felt bashful and let her pass. But the Birch made way before the Brook asked. 'He, he, he,' laughed the Brook, as she grew larger. 'Ha, ha, ha,' laughed the Brook again, pushing Heather and Juniper, Fir and Birch, forwards and backwards, up and down on the great crags. The Cliff sat for many hundred years after, pondering whether it did not smile a little that day.

It was clear the Cliff did not wish to be clad. The Heather felt so vexed that she turned green again, and then she went on. 'Never mind; take courage!' said the Heather.

The Juniper sat up to look at the Heather, and at last he rose to his feet. He scratched his head a moment, and then he too went on again, and clutched so firmly, that he thought the Cliff could not help feeling it. 'If thou wilt not take me, then I will take thee,' said he. The Fir bent his toes a little to feel if they were whole, lifted one foot, which he found all right, then the other, which was all right too, and then both feet. He first examined the path he had come, then where he had been lying, and at last where he had to go. Then he strode onwards, just as though he had never fallen. The Birch had been splashed very badly, but now she got up and made herself tidy. And so they went rapidly on, upwards and sidewards, in sunshine and rain. 'But what in the world is all this?' said the Cliff, when the summer sun shone, the dew-drops glittered, the birds sang, the wood-mouse squeaked, the hare bounded, and the weasel hid and screamed among the trees.

Then the day came when the Heather could peep over the Cliff's edge. 'Oh, dear me!' said she, and over she went. 'What is it the Heather sees, dear?' said the Juniper, and came forwards till he, too, could peep over. 'Dear me!' he cried, and over he went. 'What's the matter with the Juniper to-day?' said the Fir, taking long strides in the hot sun. Soon he, too, by standing on tiptoes could peep over. 'Ah...' Every branch and prickle stood on end with astonishment. He strode onwards, and over he went. 'What is it they all see, and not I?' said the Birch, lifting up her skirts, and tripping after. 'Ah!' said she, putting her head over, 'there is a whole forest, both of Fir and Heather, and Juniper and Birch, waiting for us on the plain;' and her leaves trembled in the sunshine till the dew-drops fell. 'This comes of reaching forwards,' said the Juniper.

II.

A CLOUDY DAWN

Arne was born upon the mountain plain.

His mother's name was Margit, and she was the only child at the farm, Kampen. In her eighteenth year she once stayed too long at a dancing party. The friends she came with had left, and then she thought the way homewards would be just the same whether she stayed over another dance or not. So it came to pass that she was still sitting there when the fiddler, Nils, the tailor, laid aside his violin and asked another man to play. He then took out the prettiest girl to dance, his feet keeping as exact time as the music to a song, while with his boot-heel he kicked off the hat of the tallest man there. 'Ho!' he said.

As Margit walked home that night, the moonbeams played upon the snow with such strange beauty, that after she had gone up to her bedchamber she felt she must look out at them once more. She took off her bodice, but remained standing with it in her hand. Then she felt chilly, undressed herself hastily, and crouched far down beneath the fur coverlet. That night she dreamed of a great red cow which had gone astray in the corn-fields. She wished to drive it out, but however much she tried, she could not move from the spot; and the cow stood quietly, and went on eating till it grew plump and satisfied, from time to time looking over to her with its large, mild eyes.

The next time there was a dance in the parish, Margit was there. She sat listening to the music, and cared little for the dancing that night; and she was glad somebody else, too, cared no more for it than she did. But when it grew later the fiddler, Nils, the tailor, rose, and wished to dance. He went straight over and took out Margit, and before she well knew what she was doing she danced with him.

Soon the weather turned warmer, and there was no more dancing. That spring Margit took so much care of a little sick lamb, that her mother thought her quite foolish. 'It's only a lamb, after all,' said the mother. 'Yes; but it's sick,' answered Margit.

It was a long time since Margit had been to church; somebody must stay at home, she used to say, and she would rather let the mother go. One Sunday, however, later in the summer, the weather seemed so fine that the hay might very well be left over that day and night, the mother said, and she thought both of them might go. Margit had nothing to say against it, and she went to dress herself. But when they had gone far enough to hear the church bells, she suddenly burst into tears. The mother grew deadly pale; yet they went on to church, heard the sermon and prayers, sang all the hymns, and let the last sound of the bells die away before they left. But when they were seated at home again, the mother took Margit's face between her hands, and said, 'Keep back nothing from me, my child!'

When another winter came Margit did not dance. But Nils, the tailor, played and drank more than ever, and always danced with the prettiest girl at every party. People then said, in fact, he might have had any one of the first girls in the parish for his wife if he chose; and some even said that Eli Böen had himself made an offer for his daughter, Birgit, who had quite fallen in love with him.

But just at that time an infant born at Kampen was baptized, and received the name, Arne; but Nils, the tailor, was said to be its father.

On the evening of the same day, Nils went to a large wedding-party; and there he got drunk. He would not play, but danced all the time, and seemed as if he could hardly bear to have any one on the floor save himself. But when he asked Birgit Böen to dance, she refused. He gave a short, forced, laugh, turned on his heel and asked the first girl at hand. She was a little dark girl who had been sitting looking at him, but now when he spoke to her, she turned pale and drew back. He looked down, leaned slightly over her, and whispered, 'Won't you dance with me, Kari?' She did not answer. He repeated his question, and then she replied, also in a whisper, 'That dance might go further than I wished.' He drew back slowly; but when he reached the middle of the room, he made a quick turn, and danced the *halling** alone, while the rest looked on in silence.

Afterwards, he went away into the barn, lay down, and wept.

Margit stayed at home with little Arne. When she heard how Nils rushed from dancing-party to dancing-party, she looked at the child and wept, but then she looked at him once more and was happy. The first name she taught him to say was, father; but this she dared not do when the mother, or the grandmother, as she was now called, was near; and so

*   For this and subsequent notes, see the section beginning on p. 159.

it came to pass that the little one called the grandmother, 'Father.' Margit took great pains to break him of this, and thus she caused an early thoughtfulness in him. He was but a little fellow when he learned that Nils, the tailor, was his father; and just when he came to the age when children most love strange, romantic things, he also learned what sort of man Nils was. But the grandmother had strictly forbidden the very mention of his name; her mind was set only upon extending Kampen and making it their own property, so that Margit and the boy might be independent. Taking advantage of the landowner's poverty, she bought the place, paid off part of the purchase-money every year, and managed her farm like a man; for she had been a widow fourteen years. Under her care, Kampen had been extended till it could now feed four cows, sixteen sheep, and a horse of which she was joint owner.

Meantime, Nils, the tailor, continued to go about working in the parish; but he had less to do than formerly, partly because he was less attentive to his trade, and partly because he was not so well liked. Then he took to going out oftener to play the fiddle at parties; this gave him more opportunities for drinking, and thus came more fighting and miserable days.

One winter day, when Arne was about six years old, he was playing on the bed, where he had set up the coverlet for a boat-sail, while he sat steering with a ladle. The grandmother sat in the room spinning, busy with her own thoughts, and every now and then nodding, as though in affirmation of her own conclusions. Then the boy knew she was taking no notice of him; and so he sang, just as he had learned it, a wild, rough song about Nils, the tailor:

'Unless 'twas only yesterday, hither first you came,
You've surely heard already of Nils, the tailor's fame.

Unless 'twas but this morning, you came among us first,
You've heard how he knocked over tall Johan Knutson
    Kirst;

How in his famous barn-fight with Ola Stor-Johann,
He said, "Bring down your porridge when we two fight
    again.'

That fighting fellow, Bugge, a famous man was he:
His name was known all over fiord and fell and sea.

"Now, choose the place, you tailor, where I shall knock
    you down;
And then I'll spit upon it, and there I'll lay your crown."

"Ah, only come so near, I may catch your scent, my man:
Your bragging hurts nobody, don't dream it ever can."

The first round was a poor one, and neither man could
    beat;
But both kept in their places, and steady on their feet.

The second round, poor Bugge was beaten black and blue.
"Little Bugge, are you tired? It's going hard with you."

The third round, Bugge tumbled, and bleeding there he
    lay.
"Now, Bugge, where's your bragging?" "Bad luck to me
    to-day!"'

This was all the boy sang; but there were two verses more which the mother had never taught him. The grandmother knew these last verses only too well; and she remembered them all the better because the boy did not sing them. She said nothing to him, however, but to the mother, she said, 'If you think it well to teach him the first verses, don't forget to teach him the last ones, too.'

Nils, the tailor, was so broken down by his drinking, that he was not like the same man; and people began to say he would soon be utterly ruined.

About this time a wedding was celebrated in the neighbourhood, and two American gentlemen, who were visiting near, came to witness it, as they wished to see the customs of the country. Nils played; and the two gentlemen each gave a dollar for him, and then asked for the *halling*. But no one came forward to dance it; and several begged Nils himself to come: 'After all, he was still the best dancer,' they said. He refused; but their request became still more urgent, and at last all in the room joined in it. This was just what he wanted; and at once he handed his fiddle to another man, took off his jacket and cap, and stepped smilingly into the middle of the room. They all came round to look at him, just as they used to do in his better days, and this gave him back his old strength. They crowded closely together, those farthest back standing on tables and benches. Several of the girls stood higher than all the rest; and the foremost of them — a tall girl, with bright auburn hair, blue eyes, deeply set under a high forehead, and thin lips, which often smiled and then drew a little to one side — was Birgit Böen: Nils caught her eye as he glanced upwards at the beam. The music struck up; a deep silence ensued; and he began. He squatted on the floor, and hopped sidewards in time with the music; swung from one side to another, crossed, and uncrossed his legs under him several times; sprang up again, and stood as though he were going to take a leap; but then shirked it, and went on hopping sidewards as before. The fiddle was skilfully played, and the tune became more and more exciting. Nils gradually threw his head backwarder, and then suddenly kicked the beam, scattering the dust from the ceiling down upon the people below. They laughed and shouted round him, and the girls stood almost breathless. The sound of the violin rose high above the noise, stimulating him by still wilder notes, and he did not resist their influence. He bent forward; hopped in time with the music; stood up as though he were going to take a leap, but shirked it, swung from one side to the other as before; and just when he looked as if he had not the least thought of leaping, leaped up and kicked the beam again and again. Next he turned somersaults forwards and backwards, coming upon his feet firmly, and standing up quite straight each time. Then he suddenly left off; and the tune, after running through some wild variations, died away in one long, deep note on the bass. The crowd dispersed, and an animated conversation in loud tones followed the silence. Nils leaned against the wall; and the American gentlemen, with their interpreter, went over to him, each giving him five dollars. Once more all were silent.

The Americans said a few words aside to their interpreter, who then asked Nils whether he would go with them as their servant. 'Where?' Nils asked, while the people crowded round as closely as possible. 'Out into the world,' was the answer. 'When?' Nils asked, as he looked round him with a bright face; his eyes fell on Birgit Böen, and he did not take them off again. 'In a week's time when they come back here,' answered the interpreter. 'Well, perhaps I may then be ready,' said Nils, weighing his ten dollars, and trembling so violently, that a man on whose shoulder he was resting one arm, asked him to sit down.

'Oh, it's nothing,' he answered, and he took a few faltering steps across the floor, then, some firmer ones, turned round, and asked for a springing-dance.

The girls stood foremost in the circle. He looked slowly round, and then went straight over to one in a dark coloured skirt: it was Birgit Böen. He stretched forth his hand, and she gave both hers; but he drew back with a laugh, took out a girl who stood next, and danced off gaily. Birgit's face and neck flushed crimson; and in a moment a tall, mild-looking man, who was standing behind her, took her hand and danced away with her just after Nils. He saw them, and whether purposely or not, pushed against them so violently that they both fell heavily to the floor. Loud cries and laughter were heard all round. Birgit rose, went aside, and cried bitterly.

Her partner rose more slowly, and went straight over to Nils, who was still dancing: 'You must stop a little,' he said. Nils did not hear; so the other man laid hold on his arm. He tore himself away, looked at the man, and said with a smile, 'I don't know you.'

'P'r'aps not; but now I'll let you know who I am,' said the man, giving him a blow just over one eye. Nils was quite unprepared for this, and fell heavily on the sharp edge of the fireplace. He tried to rise, but he could not: his spine was broken.

At Kampen, a change had taken place. Of late the grandmother had become more infirm, and as she felt her strength failing, she took greater pains than ever to save money to pay off the remaining debt upon the farm. 'Then you and the boy,' she used to say to Margit, 'will be comfortably off. And mind, if ever you bring anybody into the place to ruin it for you, I shall turn in my grave.' In harvest-time, she had the great satisfaction of going up to the late landowner's house with the last of the money due to him; and happy she felt when, seated once more in the porch at home, she could at last say, 'Now it's done.' But in that same hour she was seized with her last illness; she went to bed at once, and rose no more. Margit had her buried in the churchyard, and a nice headstone was set over her, inscribed with her name and age, and a verse from one of Kingo's hymns. A fortnight after her burial, her black Sunday gown was made into a suit of clothes for the boy; and when he was dressed in them he became as grave as even the grandmother herself. He went of his own accord and took up the book with clasps and large print from which she used to read and sing every Sunday; he opened it, and there he found her spectacles. These he had never been allowed to touch while she was living; now he took them out half fearfully, placed them over his nose, and looked down through them into the book. All became hazy. 'How strange this is,' he thought; 'it was through them grandmother could read God's word!' He held them high up against the light to see what was the matter, and — the spectacles dropped on the floor, broken in twenty pieces.

He was much frightened, and when at the same moment the door opened, he felt as if it must be the grandmother herself who was coming in. But it was the mother, and behind her came six men, who, with much stamping and noise, brought in a litter which they placed in the middle of the room. The door was left open so long after them, that the room grew quite cold.

On the litter lay a man with a pale face and dark hair. The mother walked to and fro and wept. 'Be careful how you lay him on the bed,' she said imploringly, helping them herself. But all the while the men were moving him, something grated beneath their feet. 'Ah, that's only grandmother's spectacles,' the boy thought; but he said nothing.

III.

SEEING AN OLD LOVE

It was, as we have said before, just harvest-time. A week after the day when Nils had been carried into Margit Kampen's house, the American gentlemen sent him word to get ready to go with them. He was just then lying writhing under a violent attack of pain; and, clenching his teeth, he cried, 'Let them go to the devil!' Margit remained waiting, as if she had not received any answer; he noticed this, and after a while he repeated, faintly and slowly, 'Let them — go.'

As the winter advanced, he recovered so far as to be able to get up, though his health was broken for life. The first day he could get up he took his fiddle and tuned it; but it excited him so much that he had to go to bed again. He talked very little, but was gentle and kind, and soon he began to read with Arne, and to take in work. Still he never went out; and he did not talk to those who came to see him. At first Margit used to tell him the news of the parish, but it made him gloomy, and so she soon left off.

When spring came he and Margit often sat longer than usual talking together after supper, when Arne had been sent to bed. Later in the season the banns of marriage were published for them, and then they were quietly married.

He worked on the farm, and managed wisely and steadily; and Margit said to Arne, 'He is industrious, as well as pleasant; now you must be obedient and kind, and do your best for him.'

Margit had even in the midst of her trouble remained tolerably stout. She had rosy cheeks, large eyes, surrounded by dark circles which made them seem still larger, full lips, and a round face; and she looked healthy and strong, although she really had not much strength. Now, she looked better than ever; and she always sang at her work, just as she used to do.

Then one Sunday afternoon, the father and son went out to see how things were getting on in the fields. Arne ran about, shooting with a bow and arrows, which the father had himself made for him. Thus, they went on straight towards the road which led past the church, and down to the place which was called the broad valley. When they came there, Nils sat down on a stone and fell into a reverie, while Arne went on shooting, and running for his arrows along the road in the direction of the church. 'Only not too far away,' Nils said. Just as Arne was at the height of his play, he stopped, listening, and called out, 'Father, I hear music.' Nils, too, listened; and they heard the sound of violins, sometimes drowned by loud, wild shouts, while above all rose the rattling of wheels, and the trampling of horses' hoofs: it was a bridal train coming home from the church. 'Come here, lad,' the father said, in a tone which made Arne feel he must come quickly. The father had risen hastily, and now stood hidden behind a large tree. Arne followed till the father called out, 'Not here, but go yonder!' Then the boy ran behind an elm-copse. The train of carriages had already turned the corner of the birch-wood; the horses, white with foam, galloping at a furious rate, while drunken people shouted and hallooed. The father and Arne counted the carriages one after another: there were fourteen. In the first, two fiddlers were sitting; and the wedding tune sounded merrily through the clear air: a lad stood behind driving. In the next carriage sat the bride, with her crown and ornaments glittering in the sunshine. She was tall, and when she smiled her mouth drew a little to one side; with her sat a mild-looking man, dressed in blue. Then came the rest of the carriages, the men sitting on the women's laps, and little boys behind; drunken men riding six together in a one-horse carriage; while in the last sat the purveyor of the feast, with a cask of brandy in his arms. They drove rapidly past Nils and Arne, shouting and singing down the hill; while behind them the breeze bore upwards, through a cloud of dust, the sound of the violins, the cries, and the rattling of the wheels, at first loud, then fainter and fainter, till at last it died away in the distance. Nils remained standing motionless till he heard a little rustling behind him; then he turned round: it was Arne stealing forth from his hiding-place.

'Who was it, father?' he asked; but then he started back a little, for Nils' face had an evil look. The boy stood silently, waiting for an answer; but he got none; and at last, becoming impatient, he ventured to ask, 'Are we going now?' Nils was still standing motionless, looking dreamily in the direction where the bridal train had gone; then he collected himself, and walked homewards. Arne followed, and once more began to shoot and to run after his arrows. 'Don't trample down the meadow,' said Nils abruptly. The boy let the arrow lie and came back; but soon he forgot the warning, and, while the father once more stood still, he lay down to make somersaults. 'Don't trample down the meadow, I say,' repeated Nils, seizing his arm and snatching him up by it almost violently enough to sprain it. Then the boy went on silently behind him.

At the door Margit stood waiting for them. She had just come from the cow-house, where it seemed she had been working hard, for her hair was rough, her linen soiled, and her dress untidy; but she stood in the doorway smiling. 'Red-side has calved,' she said; 'and never in all my life did I see such a great calf.' Away rushed Arne.

'I think you might make yourself a little tidy of a Sunday,' said Nils as he went past her into the room.

'Yes, now the work's done, there'll be time for dressing,' answered Margit, following him: and she began to dress, singing meanwhile. Margit now sang very well, though sometimes her voice was a little hoarse.

'Leave off that screaming,' said Nils, throwing himself upon the bed. Margit left off. Then the boy came bustling in, all out of breath. 'The calf, the calf's got red marks on each side and a spot on the forehead, just like his mother.'

'Hold your tongue, boy!' cried Nils, putting down one of his feet from the bed, and stamping on the floor. 'The deuce is in that bustling boy,' he growled out, drawing up his foot again.

'You can see very well father's out of spirits to-day,' the mother said to Arne, by way of warning. 'Shouldn't you like some strong coffee with treacle?' she then said, turning to Nils, trying to drive away his ill-temper. Coffee with treacle had been a favourite drink with the grandmother and Margit, and Arne liked it too. But Nils never liked it, though he used to take it with the others. 'Shouldn't you like some strong coffee with treacle?' Margit asked again, for he did not answer the first time. Now, he raised himself on his elbows, and cried in a loud, harsh voice, 'Do you think I'll guzzle that filthy stuff?'

Margit was thunder-struck; and she went out, taking the boy with her.

They had several things to do out-doors, and they did not come in till supper-time; then Nils had gone. Arne was sent out into the field to call him, but could not find him anywhere. They waited till the supper was nearly cold; but Nils had not come even when it was finished. Then Margit grew fidgety, sent Arne to bed, and sat down, waiting. A little past midnight Nils came home. 'Where have you been, dear?' she asked.

'That's no business of yours,' he answered, seating himself slowly on the bench. He was drunk.

From that time he often went out into the parish; and he was always drunk when he came back. 'I can't bear stopping at home with you,' he once said when he came in. She gently tried to plead her cause; but he stamped on the floor, and bade her be silent. Was he drunk, then it was her fault; was he wicked, that was her fault, too; had he become a cripple and an unlucky man for all his life, then, again, she and that cursed boy of hers were the cause of it. 'Why were you always dangling after me?' he said, blubbering. 'What harm had I done you?'

'God help and bless me!' Margit answered, 'was it I that ran after you?'

'Yes, that you did,' he cried, raising himself; and, still blubbering, he continued, 'Now, at last, it has turned out just as you would have it: I drag along here day after day — every day looking on my own grave. But I might have lived in splendour with the first girl in the parish; I might have travelled as far as the sun; if you and that cursed boy of yours hadn't put yourselves in my way.'

Again she tried to defend herself: 'It isn't the boy's fault, at any rate.'

'Hold your tongue, or I'll strike you!' and he did strike her.

The next day, when he had slept himself sober, he felt ashamed, and would especially be kind to the boy. But he was soon drunk again; and then he beat Margit. At last he beat her almost every time he was drunk; Arne then cried and fretted, and so he beat him, too; but often he was so miserable afterwards that he felt obliged to go out again and take some more spirits. At this time, too, he began once more to set his mind on going to dancing-parties. He played at them just as he used to do before his illness; and he took Arne with him to carry the fiddle-case. At these parties the child saw and heard much which was not good for him; and the mother often wept because he was taken there: still she dared not say anything to the father about it. But to the child she often imploringly said, with many caresses, 'Keep close to God, and don't learn anything wicked.' But at the dancing-parties there was very much to amuse him, while at home with the mother there was very little; and so he turned more and more away from her to the father: she saw it, but was silent. He learned many songs at these parties, and he used to sing them to the father, who felt amused, and laughed now and then at them. This flattered the boy so much that he set himself to learn as many songs as he could; and soon he found out what it was that the father liked, and that made him laugh. When there was nothing of this kind in the songs, the boy would himself put something in as well as he could; and thus he early acquired facility in setting words to music. But lampoons and disgusting stories about people who had risen to wealth and influence, were the things which the father liked best, and which the boy sang.

The mother always wished him to go with her in the cow-house to tend the cattle in the evening. He used to find all sorts of excuses to avoid going; but it was of no use; she was resolved he should go. There she talked to him about God and good things, and generally ended by pressing him to her heart, imploring him, with many tears, not to become a bad man.

She helped him, too, in his reading-lessons. He was extremely quick in learning; and the father felt proud of him, and told him — especially when he was drunk — that he had his cleverness.

At dancing-parties, when the father was drunk, he used often to ask Arne to sing to the people; and then he would sing song after song, amidst their loud laughter and applause. This pleased him even more than it pleased his father; and at last he used to sing songs without number. Some anxious mothers who heard this, came to Margit and told her about it, because the subjects of the songs were not such as they ought to have been. Then she called the boy to her side, and forbade him, in the name of God and all that was good, to sing such songs any more. And now it seemed to him that she was always opposed to what gave him pleasure; and, for the first time in his life, he told the father what she had said; and when he was again drunk she had to suffer for it severely: till then he had not spoken of it. Then Arne saw clearly how wrong a thing he had done, and in the depths of his soul he asked God and her to forgive him; but he could not ask it in words. She continued to show him the same kindness as before, and it pierced his heart. Once, however, in spite of all, he again wronged her. He had a talent for mimicking people, especially in their speaking and singing; and one evening, while he was amusing the father in this way, the mother entered, and, when she was going away, the father took it into his head to ask him to mimic her. At first he refused; but the father, who lay on the bed laughing till he shook, insisted upon his doing it. 'She's gone,' the boy thought, 'and can't hear me;' and he mimicked her singing, just as it was when her voice was hoarse and obstructed by tears. The father laughed till the boy grew quite frightened and at once left off. Then the mother came in from the kitchen, looked at Arne long and mournfully, went over to the shelf, took down a milk-dish and carried it away.

He felt burning hot all over: she had heard it all. He jumped down from the table where he had been sitting, went out, threw himself on the ground, and wished to hide himself for ever in the earth. He could not rest, and he rose and went farther from the house. Passing by the barn, he there saw his mother sitting, making a new fine shirt for him. It was her usual habit to sing a hymn while sewing: now, however, she was silent. Then Arne could bear it no longer; he threw himself on the grass at her feet, looked up in her face, and wept and sobbed bitterly. Margit let fall her work, and took his head between her hands.

'Poor Arne!' she said, putting her face down to his. He did not try to say a word, but wept as he had never wept before. 'I knew you were good at heart,' she said, stroking his head.

'Mother, you mustn't refuse what I am now going to ask,' were the first words he was able to utter.

'You know I never do refuse you,' answered she.

He tried to stop his tears, and then, with his face still in her lap, he stammered out, 'Do sing a little for me, mother.'

'You know I can't do it,' she said, in a low voice.

'Sing something for me, mother,' implored the boy; 'or I shall never have courage to look you in the face again.' She went on stroking his hair, but was silent. 'Do sing, mother dear,' he implored again; 'or I shall go far away, and never come back any more.' Though he was now almost fifteen years old, he lay there with his head in his mother's lap, and she began to sing:

'Merciful Father, take in thy care
The child as he plays by the shore;
Send him Thy Holy Spirit there,
And leave him alone no more.
Slipp'ry's the way, and high is the tide;
Still if Thou keepest close by his side
He never will drown, but live for Thee,
And then at the last Thy heaven will see.

'Wondering where her child is astray,
The mother stands at the cottage door,
Calls him a hundred times i' the day,
And fears he will come no more.
But then she thinks, whatever betide,
The Spirit of God will be his Guide,

And Christ the blessèd, his little Brother,
Will carry him back to his longing mother.'

She sang some more verses. Arne lay still; a blessed peace came over him, and under its soothing influence he slept. The last word he heard distinctly was, 'Christ;' it transported him into regions of light; and he fancied that he listened to a chorus of voices, but his mother's voice was clearer than all. Sweeter tones he had never heard, and he prayed to be allowed to sing in like manner; and then at once he began, gently and softly, and still more softly, until his bliss became rapture, and then suddenly all disappeared. He awoke, looked about him, listened attentively, but heard nothing save the little rivulet which flowed past the barn with a low and constant murmur. The mother was gone; but she had placed the half-made shirt and his jacket under his head.

IV.

THE UNLAMENTED DEATH

When now the time of year came for the cattle to be sent into the wood, Arne wished to go to tend them. But the father opposed him: indeed, he had never gone before, though he was now in his fifteenth year. But he pleaded so well, that his wish was at last complied with; and so during the spring, summer, and autumn, he passed the whole day alone in the wood, and only came home to sleep.

He took his books up there, and read, carved letters in the bark of the trees, thought, longed, and sang. But when in the evening he came home and found the father often drunk and beating the mother, cursing her and the whole parish, and saying how once he might have gone far away, then a longing for travelling arose in the lad's mind. There was no comfort for him at home; and his books made his thoughts travel; nay, it seemed sometimes as if the very breeze bore them on its wings far away.

Then, about midsummer, he met with Christian, the Captain's eldest son, who one day came to the wood with the servant boy, to catch the horses, and to ride them home. He was a few years older than Arne, light-hearted and jolly, restless in mind, but nevertheless strong in purpose; he spoke fast and abruptly, and generally about two things at once; shot birds in their flight; rode bare-backed horses; went fly-fishing; and altogether seemed to Arne the paragon of perfection. He, too, had set his mind upon travelling, and he talked to Arne about foreign countries till they shone like fairy-lands. He found out Arne's love for reading, and he carried up to him all the books he had read himself; on Sundays he taught him geography from maps: and during the whole of that summer Arne read till he became pale and thin.

Even when the winter came, he was permitted to read at home; partly because he was going to be confirmed the next year, and partly because he always knew how to manage with his father. He also began to go to school; but while there it seemed to him he never got on so well as when he shut his eyes and thought over the things in his books at home: and he no longer had any companions among the boys of the parish.

The father's bodily infirmity, as well as his passion for drinking, increased with his years; and he treated his wife worse and worse. And while Arne sat at home trying to amuse him, and often, merely to keep peace for the mother, telling things which he now despised, a hatred of his father grew up in his heart. But there he kept it secretly, just as he kept his love for his mother. Even when he happened to meet Christian, he said nothing to him about home affairs; but all their talk ran upon their books and their intended travels. But often when, after those wide roaming conversations, he was returning home alone, thinking of what he perhaps would have to see when he arrived there, he wept and prayed that God would take care he might soon be allowed to go away.

In the summer he and Christian were confirmed: and soon afterwards the latter carried out his purpose of travelling. At last, he prevailed upon his father to let him be a sailor; and he went far away; first giving Arne his books, and promising to write often to him.

Then Arne was left alone.

About this time a wish to make songs awoke again in his mind; and now he no longer patched old songs, but made new ones for himself, and said in them whatever most pained him.

But soon his heart became too heavy to let him make songs any more. He lay sleepless whole nights, feeling that he could not bear to stay at home any longer, and that he must go far away, find out Christian, and — not say a word about it to any one. But when he thought of the mother, and what would become of her, he could scarcely look her in the face; and his love made him linger still.

One evening when it was growing late, Arne sat reading: indeed, when he felt more sad than usual he always took refuge in his books; little understanding that they only increased his burden. The father had gone to a wedding party, but was expected home that evening; the mother, weary and afraid of him, had gone to bed. Then Arne was startled by the sound of a heavy fall in the passage, and of something hard pushing against the door. It was the father, just coming home.

'Is it you, my clever boy?' he muttered; 'come and help your father to get up.' Arne helped him up, and brought him to the bench; then carried in the violin-case after him, and shut the door. 'Well, look at me, you clever boy; I don't look very handsome now; Nils, the tailor's no longer the man he used to be. One thing I — tell — you — you shall never drink spirits; they're — the devil, the world, and the flesh... "God resisteth the proud, but giveth grace to the humble..." Oh dear! oh dear! — How far gone I am!'

He sat silent for a while, and then sang in a tearful voice,

'Merciful Lord, I come to Thee;
Help, if there can be help for me;
Though by the mire of sin defiled,
I'm still Thine own dear ransomed child.'

"'Lord, I am not worthy that Thou shouldest come under my roof; but speak the word only..." He threw himself forward, hid his face in his hands, and sobbed violently. Then, after lying thus a long while, he said, word for word out of the Scriptures, just as he had learned it more than twenty years ago, "'But he answered and said, I am not sent but unto the lost sheep of the house of Israel. Then came she and worshipped him, saying, Lord, help me. But he answered and said, It is not meet to take the children's bread, and to cast it to dogs. And she said, Truth, Lord: yet the dogs eat of the crumbs which fall from their master's table."

Then he was silent, and his weeping became subdued and calm.

The mother had been long awake, without looking up; but now when she heard him weeping thus like one who is saved, she raised herself on her elbows, and gazed earnestly at him.

But scarcely did Nils perceive her before he called out, 'Are you looking up, you ugly vixen! I suppose you would like to see what a state you have brought me to. Well, so I look, just so!' He rose; and she hid herself under the fur coverlet. 'Nay, don't hide, I'm sure to find you,' he said, stretching out his right hand and fumbling with his forefinger on the bed-clothes, 'Tickle, tickle,' he said, turning aside the fur coverlet, and putting his forefinger on her throat.

'Father!' cried Arne.

'How shrivelled and thin you've become already, there's no depth of flesh here!' She writhed beneath his touch, and seized his hand with both hers, but could not free herself.

'Father!' repeated Arne.

'Well at last you're roused. How she wriggles, the ugly thing! Can't you scream to make believe I am beating you? Tickle, tickle! I only want to take away your breath.'

'Father!' Arne said once more, running to the corner of the room, and snatching up an axe which stood there.

'Is it only out of perverseness, you don't scream? you had better beware; for I've taken such a strange fancy into my head. Tickle, tickle! Now I think I shall soon get rid of that screaming of yours.'

'Father!' Arne shouted, rushing towards him with the axe uplifted.

But before Arne could reach him, he started up with a piercing cry, laid his hand upon his heart, and fell heavily down. 'Jesus Christ!' he muttered, and then lay quite still.

Arne stood as if rooted in the ground, and gradually lowered the axe. He grew dizzy and bewildered, and scarcely knew where he was. Then the mother began to move to and fro in the bed, and to breathe heavily, as if oppressed by some great weight lying upon her. Arne saw that she needed help; but yet he felt unable to render it. At last she raised herself a little, and saw the father lying stretched on the floor, and Arne standing beside him with the axe.

41

'Merciful Lord, what have you done?' she cried, springing out of the bed, putting on her skirt and coming nearer.

'He fell down himself,' said Arne, at last regaining power to speak.

'Arne, Arne, I don't believe you,' said the mother in a stern reproachful voice: 'now Jesus help you!' And she threw herself upon the dead man with loud wailing.

But the boy awoke from his stupor, dropped the axe and fell down on his knees: 'As true as I hope for mercy from God, I've not done it. I almost thought of doing it; I was so bewildered; but then he fell down himself; and here I've been standing ever since.'

The mother looked at him, and believed him. 'Then our Lord has been here Himself,' she said quietly, sitting down on the floor and gazing before her.

Nils lay quite stiff, with open eyes and mouth, and hands drawn near together, as though he had at the last moment tried to fold them, but had been unable to do so. The first thing the mother now did was to fold them. 'Let us look closer at him,' she said then, going over to the fireplace, where the fire was almost out. Arne followed her, for he felt afraid of standing alone. She gave him a lighted fir-splinter to hold; then she once more went over to the dead body and stood by one side of it, while the son stood at the other, letting the light fall upon it.

'Yes, he's quite gone,' she said; and then, after a little while, she continued, 'and gone in an evil hour, I'm afraid.'

Arne's hands trembled so much that the burning ashes of the splinter fell upon the father's clothes and set them on fire; but the boy did not perceive it, neither did the mother at first, for she was weeping. But soon she became aware of it through the bad smell, and she cried out in fear. When now the boy looked, it seemed to him as though the father himself was burning, and he dropped the splinter upon him, sinking down in a swoon. Up and down, and round and round, the room moved with him; the table moved, the bed moved; the axe hewed; the father rose and came to him; and then all of them came rolling upon him. Then he felt as if a soft cooling breeze passed over his face; and he cried out and awoke. The first thing he did was to look at the father, to assure himself that he still lay quietly.

And a feeling of inexpressible happiness came over the boy's mind when he saw that the father was dead — really dead; and he rose as though he were entering upon a new life.

The mother had extinguished the burning clothes, and began to lay out the body. She made the bed, and then said to Arne, 'Take hold of your father, you're so strong, and help me to lay him nicely.' They laid him on the bed, and Margit shut his eyes and mouth, stretched his limbs, and folded his hands once more.

Then they both stood looking at him. It was only a little past midnight, and they had to stay there with him till morning. Arne made a good fire, and the mother sat down by it. While sitting there, she looked back upon the many miserable days she had passed with Nils, and she thanked God for taking him away. 'But still I had some happy days with him, too,' she said after a while.

Arne took a seat opposite her; and, turning to him, she went on, 'And to think that he should have such an end as this! even if he has not lived as he ought, truly he has suffered for it.' She wept, looked over to the dead man, and continued, 'But now God grant I may be repaid for all I have gone through with him. Arne, you must remember it was for your sake I suffered it all.' The boy began to weep too. 'Therefore, you must never leave me,' she sobbed; 'you are now my only comfort.'

'I never will leave you; that I promise before God,' the boy said, as earnestly as if he had thought of saying it for years. He felt a longing to go over to her; yet he could not.

She grew calmer, and, looking kindly over at the dead man, she said, 'After all, there was a great deal of good in him; but the world dealt hardly by him... But now he's gone to our Lord, and He'll be kinder to him, I'm sure.' Then, as if she had been following out this thought within herself, she added, 'We must pray for him. If I could, I would sing over him; but you, Arne, have such a fine voice, you must go and sing to your father.'

Arne fetched the hymn-book and lighted a fir-splinter; and, holding it in one hand and the book in the other, he went to the head of the bed and sang in a clear voice Kingo's 127th hymn:

'Regard us again in mercy, O God!
And turn Thou aside Thy terrible rod,
That now in Thy wrath laid on us we see
To chasten us sore for sin against Thee.'

V.

'HE HAD IN HIS MIND A SONG.'

Arne was now in his twentieth year. Yet he continued tending the cattle upon the mountains in the summer, while in the winter he remained at home studying.

About this time the clergyman sent a message, asking him to become the parish schoolmaster, and saying his gifts and knowledge might thus be made useful to his neighbours. Arne sent no answer; but the next day, while he was driving his flock, he made the following verses:

'O, my pet lamb, lift your head,Though a stony path you tread,Over all the lonely fells,Only follow still your bells.

O, my pet lamb, walk with care;
Lest you spoil your wool, beware:
Mother now must soon be sewing
New lamb-skins, for summer's going.

O, my pet lamb, try to grow
Fat and fine where'er you go:
Know you not, my little sweeting,
A spring-lamb is dainty eating?'

One day he happened to overhear a conversation between his mother and the late owner of the place: they were at odds about the horse of which they were joint-owners. 'I must wait and hear what Arne says,' interposed the mother. 'That sluggard!' the man exclaimed; 'he would like the horse to ramble about in the wood, just as he does himself.' Then the mother became silent, though before she had been pleading her cause well.

Arne flushed crimson. That his mother had to bear people's jeers on his account, never before occurred to him, and, 'Perhaps she had borne many,' he thought. 'But why had she not told him of it?' he thought again.

He turned the matter over, and then it came into his mind that the mother scarcely ever talked to him at all. But, then, he scarcely ever talked to her either. But, after all, whom did he talk much to?

Often on Sundays, when he was sitting quietly at home, he would have liked to read the sermon to his mother, whose eyes were weak, for she had wept too much in her time. Still, he did not read it. Often, too, on weekdays, when she was sitting down, and he thought the time might hang heavy, he would have liked to offer to read some of his own books to her: still, he did not.

'Well, never mind,' thought he: 'I'll soon leave off tending the cattle on the mountains; and then I'll be more with mother.' He let this resolve ripen within him for several days: meanwhile he drove his cattle far about in the wood, and made the following verses:

'The vale is full of trouble, but here sweet Peace may
    reign;
Within this quiet forest no bailiffs may distrain;
None fight, like all in the vale, in the Blessèd Church's

name;
But still if a church were here, perhaps 'twould be just the
   same.

Here all are at peace — true, the hawk is rather unkind;
I fear he is looking now the plumpest sparrow to find;
I fear yon eagle is coming to rob the kid of his breath;
But still if he lived very long he might be tired to death.

The woodman fells one tree, and another rots away:
The red fox killed the lambkin at sunset yesterday;
But the wolf killed the fox; and the wolf, too, had to die,
For Arne shot him down to-day before the dew was dry.

Back I'll go to the valley: the forest is just as bad —
I must take heed, however, or thinking will drive me mad.
I saw a boy in my dreams, though where I cannot tell —
But I know he had killed his father, and I think it was in
   hell.'

Then he went home and told the mother she might send
for a lad to tend the cattle on the mountains; and that he
would himself manage the farm: and so it was arranged. But
the mother was constantly hovering about him, warning him
not to work too hard. Then, too, she used to get him such
nice meals that he often felt quite ashamed to take them; yet
he said nothing.

He had in his mind a song having for its burden, 'Over the
mountains high;' but he never could complete it, principally
because he always tried to bring the burden in every
alternate line; so afterwards he gave this up.

But several of his songs became known, and were much liked; and many people, especially those who had known him from his childhood, were fond of talking to him. But he was shy to all whom he did not know, and he thought ill of them, mainly because he fancied they thought ill of him.

In the next field to his own worked a middle-aged man named Opplands-Knut, who used sometimes to sing, but always the same song. After Arne had heard him singing it for several months, he thought he would ask him whether he did not know any others. 'No,' Knut answered. Then after a few more days, when he was again singing his song, Arne asked him, 'How came you to learn that one song?'

'Ah! it happened thus—' and then he said no more.

Arne went away from him straight indoors; and there he found his mother weeping; a thing he had not seen her do ever since the father's death. He turned back again, just as though he did not notice it; but he felt the mother was looking sorrowfully after him, and he was obliged to stop.

'What are you crying for, mother?' he asked. She did not answer, and all was silent in the room. Then his words came back to him again, and he felt they had not been spoken so kindly as they ought; and once more, in a gentler tone, he asked, 'What are you crying for, mother?'

'Ah, I hardly know,' she said, weeping still more. He stood silent a while; but at last mustered courage to say, 'Still, there must be some reason why you are crying.'

Again there was silence; but although the mother had not said one word of blame, he felt he was very guilty towards her. 'Well it just came over me,' she said after a while; and in a few moments she added, 'but really, I'm very happy;' and then she began weeping again.

Arne hurried out, away to the ravine; and while he sat there looking into it, he, too, began weeping. 'If I only knew what I am crying for,' he said.

Then he heard Opplands-Knut singing in the fields above him:

"Ingerid Sletten of Willow-pool
Had no costly trinkets to wear;
But a cap she had that was far more fair,
Although 'twas only of wool.

It had no trimming, and now was old;
But her mother, who long had gone,
Had given it her, and so it shone
To Ingerid more than gold.

For twenty years she laid it aside,
That it might not be worn away:
"My cap I'll wear on that blissful day
When I shall become a bride."

For thirty years she laid it aside
Lest the colours might fade away:
"My cap I'll wear when to God I pray,
A happy and grateful bride."

For forty years she laid it aside,
Still holding her mother as dear:
"My little cap, I certainly fear
I never shall be a bride."

She went to look for the cap one day
In the chest where it long had lain;

49

But, ah! her looking was all in vain:
The cap had mouldered away.'

Arne listened, and the words seemed to him like music playing far away over the mountains. He went up to Knut and asked him, 'Have you a mother?'

'No.'

'Have you a father?'

'Ah, no; no father.'

'Is it long since they died?'

'Ah, yes; it's long since.'

'You haven't many, I dare say, who love you?'

'Ah, no; not many.'

'Have you any here at all?'

'No; not here.'

'But away in your own place?'

'Ah, no; not there either.'

'Haven't you any at all then who love you?'

'Ah, no; I haven't any.'

But Arne walked away with his heart so full of love to his mother that it seemed as if it would burst; and all around him grew bright. He felt he must go in again, if only for the sake of looking at her. As he walked on the thought struck him, 'What if I were to lose her?' He stopped suddenly. 'Almighty God, what would then become of me?'

Then he felt as if some dreadful accident was happening at home, and he hurried onwards, cold drops bursting from his brow, and his feet hardly touching the ground. He threw open the outer door, and came at once into an atmosphere of peace. Then he gently opened the door of the inner room.

The mother had gone to bed, and lay sleeping as calmly as a child, with the moonbeams shining full on her face.

VI.

STRANGE TALES

A few days after, the mother and son agreed on going together to the wedding of some relations in one of the neighbouring places. The mother had not been to a party ever since she was a girl; and both she and Arne knew but very little of the people living around, save their names.

Arne felt uncomfortable at this party, however, for he fancied everybody was staring at him: and once, as he was passing through the passage, he believed he heard something said about him, the mere thought of which made every drop of blood rush into his face.

He kept going about looking after the man who had said it, and at last he took a seat next him.

When they were at dinner, the man said, 'Well, now, I shall tell you a story which proves nothing can be buried so deeply that it won't one day be brought to light;' and Arne fancied he looked at him all the time he was saying this. He was an ugly-looking man, with scanty red hair, hanging about a wide, round forehead, small, deep-set eyes, a little snub-nose, and a large mouth, with pale out-turned lips, which showed both his gums when he laughed. His hands were resting on the table; they were large and coarse, but the wrists were slender. He had a fierce look; and he spoke quickly, but with difficulty. The people called him 'Bragger;' and Arne knew that in bygone days, Nils, the tailor, had treated him badly.

'Yes,' continued the man, 'there is indeed, a great deal of sin in the world; and it sits nearer to us than we think... But never mind; I'll tell you now of a foul deed. Those of you who are old will remember Alf — Alf, the pedlar. "I'll call again," Alf used to say: and he has left that saying behind him. When he had struck a bargain — and what a fellow for trade he was! — he would take up his bundle, and say, "I'll call again." A devil of a fellow, proud fellow, brave fellow, was he, Alf, the pedlar!

'Well he and Big Lazy-bones, Big Lazy-bones — well, you know Big Lazy-bones? — big he was, and lazy he was, too. He took a fancy to a coal-black horse that Alf, the pedlar, used to drive, and had trained to hop like a summer frog. And almost before Big Lazy-bones knew what he was about, he paid fifty dollars for this horse! Then Big Lazy-bones, tall as he was, got into a carriage, meaning to drive about like a king with his fifty-dollar-horse; but, though he whipped and swore like a devil, the horse kept running against all the doors and windows; for it was stone-blind!

'Afterwards, whenever Alf and Big Lazy-bones came across each other, they used to quarrel and fight about this horse like two dogs. Big Lazy-bones said he would have his money back; but he could not get a farthing of it: and Alf drubbed him till the bristles flew. "I'll call again," said Alf. A devil of a fellow, proud fellow, brave fellow that Alf — Alf, the pedlar!

'Well, after that some years passed away without his being seen again.

'Then, in about ten years or so, a call for him was published on the church-hill,* for a great fortune had been left him. Big Lazy-bones stood listening. "Ah," said he, "I well knew it must be money, and not men, that called out for Alf, the pedlar.'

'Now, there was a good deal of talk one way and another about Alf; and at last it seemed to be pretty clearly made out that he had been seen for the last time on this side of the ledge, and not on the other. Well, you remember the road over the ledge — the old road?

'Of late, Big Lazy-bones had got quite a great man, and he owned both houses and land. Then, too, he had taken to being religious; and that, everybody knew, he didn't take to for nothing — nobody does. People began to whisper about these things.

'Just at this time the road over the ledge had to be altered. Folks in bygone days had a great fancy for going straight onwards; and so the old road ran straight over the ledge; but now-a-days we like to have things smooth and easy; and so the new road was made to run down along the river. While they were making it, there was digging and mining enough to bring down the whole mountain about their ears; and the magistrates and all the officers who have to do with that sort of thing were there. One day while the men were digging deep in the stony ground, one of them took up something which he thought was a stone; but it turned out to be the bones of a man's hand instead; and a wonderfully strong hand it seemed to be, for the man who got it fell flat down directly. That man was Big Lazy-bones. The magistrate was just strolling about round there, and they fetched him to the place; and then all the bones belonging to

54

a whole man were dug out. The Doctor, too, was fetched; and he put them all together so cleverly that nothing was wanting but the flesh. And then it struck some of the people that the skeleton was just about the same size and make as Alf, the pedlar. "I'll call again," Alf used to say.

'And then it struck somebody else, that it was a very queer thing a dead hand should have made a great fellow like Big Lazy-bones fall flat down like that: and the magistrate accused him straight of having had more to do with that dead hand than he ought — of course, when nobody else was by. But then Big Lazy-bones foreswore it with such fearful oaths that the magistrate turned quite giddy. "Well," said the magistrate, "if you didn't do it, I dare say you're a fellow, now, who would not mind sleeping with the skeleton to-night?" "No; I shouldn't mind a bit — not I," said Big Lazy-bones. So the Doctor tied the joints of the skeleton together, and laid it in one of the beds in the barracks; and put another bed close by it for Big Lazy-bones. The magistrate wrapped himself in his cloak, and lay down close to the door outside. When night came on, and Big Lazy-bones had to go in to his bedfellow, the door shut behind him as though of itself, and he stood in the dark. But then Big Lazy-bones set off singing psalms, for he had a mighty voice. "Why are you singing psalms?" the magistrate asked from outside the wall. "May be the bells were never tolled for him," answered Big Lazy-bones. Then he began praying out loud, as earnestly as ever he could. "Why are you praying?" asked the magistrate from outside the wall. "No doubt, he has been a great sinner," answered Big Lazy-bones. Then a time after, all got so still that the magistrate might have gone to sleep. But then came a shrieking that made the very barracks shake: "I'll call again!" Then came a hellish noise and crash. "Out with that fifty dollars of mine!" roared Big Lazy-bones: and the shrieking and crashing came again. Then the magistrate burst open the door; the people rushed in with poles and firebrands; and there lay Big Lazy-bones on the floor, with the skeleton on the top of him.'

There was a deep silence all round the table. At last a man who was lighting his clay-pipe said, 'Didn't he go mad from that very time?'

'Yes, he did.'

Arne fancied everybody was looking at him, and he dared not raise his eyes. 'I say, as I said before,' continued the man who had told the tale, 'nothing can be buried so deeply that it won't one day be brought to light.'

'Well, now I'll tell you about a son who beat his own father,' said a fair stout man with a round face. Arne no longer knew where he was sitting.

'This son was a great fellow, almost a giant, belonging to a tall family in Hardanger; and he was always at odds with somebody or other. He and his father were always quarrelling about the yearly allowance; and so he had no peace either at home or out.

'This made him grow more and more wicked; and the father persecuted him. "I won't be put down by anybody," the son said. "Yes, you'll be put down by me so long as I live," the father answered. "If you don't hold your tongue," said the son, rising, "I'll strike you." "Well, do if you dare; and never in this world will you have luck again," answered the father, rising also. "Do you mean to say that?" said the son; and he rushed upon him and knocked him down. But the father didn't try to help himself: he folded his arms and let the son do just as he liked with him. Then he knocked him about, rolled him over and over, and dragged him towards the door by his white hair. "I'll have peace in my own house, at any rate," said he. But when they had come to the door, the father raised himself a little and cried out, "Not beyond the door, for so far I dragged my own father." The son didn't heed it, but dragged the old man's head over the threshold. "Not beyond the door, I say!" And the old man rose, knocked down the son and beat him as one would beat a child.'

'Ah, that's a sad story,' several said. Then Arne fancied he heard some one saying, 'It's a wicked thing to strike one's father;' and he rose, turning deadly pale.

'Now I'll tell you something,' he said; but he hardly knew what he was going to say: words seemed flying around him like large snowflakes. 'I'll catch them at random,' he said and began:

'A troll once met a lad walking along the road weeping. "Whom are you most afraid of?" asked the troll, "yourself or others?" Now, the boy was weeping because he had dreamed last night he had killed his wicked father; and so he answered, "I'm most afraid of myself." "Then fear yourself no longer, and never weep again; for henceforward you shall only have strife with others." And the troll went his way. But the first whom the lad met jeered at him; and so the lad jeered at him again. The second he met beat him; and so he beat him again. The third he met tried to kill him; and so the lad killed him. Then all the people spoke ill of the lad; and so he spoke ill again of all the people. They shut the doors against him, and kept all their things away from him; so he stole what he wanted; and he even took his night's rest by stealth. As now they wouldn't let him come to do anything good, he only did what was bad; and all that was bad in other people, they let him suffer for. And the people in the place wept because of the mischief done by the lad; but he did not weep himself, for he could not. Then all the people met together and said, "Let's go and drown him, for with him we drown all the evil that is in the place." So they drowned him forthwith; but afterwards they thought the well where he was drowned gave forth a mighty odor.

'The lad himself didn't at all know he had done anything wrong; and so after his death he came drifting in to our Lord. There, sitting on a bench, he saw his father, whom he had not killed, after all; and opposite the father, on another bench, sat the one whom he had jeered at, the one he had beaten, the one he had killed, and all those whom he had stolen from, and those whom he had otherwise wronged.

'"Whom are you afraid of," our Lord asked, "of your father, or of those on the long bench?" The lad pointed to the long bench.

'"Sit down then by your father," said our Lord; and the lad went to sit down. But then the father fell down from the bench with a large axe-cut in his neck. In his seat, came one in the likeness of the lad himself, but with a thin and ghastly pale face; another with a drunkard's face, matted hair, and drooping limbs; and one more with an insane face, torn clothes, and frightful laughter.

'"So it might have happened to you," said our Lord.

'"Do you think so?" said the boy, catching hold of the Lord's coat.

'Then both the benches fell down from heaven; but the boy remained standing near the Lord rejoicing.

'"Remember this when you awake," said our Lord; and the boy awoke.

'The boy who dreamed so is I; those who tempted him by thinking him bad are you. I am no longer afraid of myself, but I am afraid of you. Do not force me to evil; for it is uncertain if I get hold of the Lord's coat.'

He ran out: the men looked at each other.

VII.

THE SOLILOQUY IN THE BARN

On the evening of the day after this, Arne was lying in a barn belonging to the same house. For the first time in his life he had become drunk, and he had been lying there for the last twenty-four hours. Now he sat up, resting upon his elbows, and talked with himself:

'...Everything I look at turns to cowardice. It was cowardice that hindered me from running away while a boy; cowardice that made me listen to father more than to mother; cowardice also made me sing the wicked songs to him. I began tending the cattle through cowardice — to read — well, that, too, was through cowardice: I wished to get away from myself. When, though a grown up lad, yet I didn't help mother against father — cowardice; that I didn't that night — ugh! — cowardice! I might perhaps have waited till she was killed! I couldn't bear to stay at home afterwards — cowardice; still I didn't go away — cowardice; I did nothing, I tended cattle... cowardice. 'Tis true I promised mother to stay at home; still I should have been cowardly enough to break my promise if I hadn't been afraid of mixing among people. For I'm afraid of people, mainly because I think they see how bad I am; and because I'm afraid of them, I speak ill of them — a curse upon my cowardice! I make songs through cowardice. I'm afraid of thinking bravely about my own affairs, and so I turn aside and think about other people's; and making verses is just that.

'I've cause enough to weep till the hills turned to lakes, but instead of that I say to myself, "Hush, hush," and begin rocking. And even my songs are cowardly; for if they were bold they would be better. I'm afraid of strong thoughts; afraid of anything that's strong; and if ever I rise into it, it's in a passion, and passion is cowardice. I'm more clever and know more than I seem; I'm better than my words, but my cowardice makes me afraid of showing myself in my true colours. Shame upon me! I drank that spirits through cowardice; I wanted to deaden my pain — shame upon me! I felt miserable all the while I was drinking it, yet I drank; drank my father's heart's-blood, and still I drank! In fact there's no end to my cowardice; and the most cowardly thing is, that I can sit and tell myself all this!

'...Kill myself? Oh, no! I am a vast deal too cowardly for that. Then, too, I believe a little in God... yes, I believe in God. I would fain go to Him; but cowardice keeps me from going: it would be such a great change that a coward shrinks from it. But if I were to put forth what power I have? Almighty God, if I tried? Thou wouldst cure me in such a way as my milky spirit can bear; wouldst lead me gently; for I have no bones in me, nor even gristle — nothing but jelly. If I tried... with good, gentle books — I'm afraid of the strong ones — with pleasant tales, stories, all that is mild, and then a sermon every Sunday, and a prayer every evening. If I tried to clear a field within me for religion; and worked in good earnest, for one cannot sow in laziness. If I tried; dear mild God of my childhood, if I tried!'

But then the barn-door was opened, and the mother came rushing across the floor. Her face was deadly pale, though the perspiration dropped from it like great tears. For the last twenty-four hours she had been rushing hither and thither, seeking her son, calling his name, and scarcely pausing even to listen, until now when he answered from the barn. Then she gave a loud cry, jumped upon the hay-mow more lightly than a boy, and threw herself upon Arne's breast...

'Arne, Arne are you here? At last I've found you; I've been looking for you ever since yesterday; I've been looking for you all night long! Poor, poor Arne! I saw they worried you, and I wanted to come to speak to you and comfort you, but really I'm always afraid!' 'Arne, I saw you drinking spirits! Almighty God, may I never see it again! Arne, I saw you drinking spirits.' It was some minutes before she was able to speak again. 'Christ have mercy upon you, my boy, I saw you drinking spirits! You were gone all at once, drunk and crushed by grief as you were! I ran all over the place; I went far into the fields; but I couldn't find you: I looked in every copse; I questioned everybody; I came here, too; but you didn't answer... Arne, Arne, I went along the river; but it seemed nowhere to be deep enough...' She pressed herself closer to him.

'Then it came into my mind all at once that you might have gone home; and I'm sure I was only a quarter of an hour going there. I opened the outer-door and looked in every room; and then, for the first time, I remembered that the house had been locked up, and I myself had the key; and that you could not have come in, after all. Arne, last night I looked all along both sides of the road: I dared not go to the edge of the ravine... I don't know how it was I came here again; nobody told me; it must have been the Lord himself who put it into my mind that you might be here!'

She paused and lay for a while with her head upon his breast.

He tried to comfort her.

'Arne, you'll never drink spirits again, I'm sure?'

'No; you may be sure I never will.'

'I believe they were very hard upon you? they were, weren't they?'

'No; it was I who was cowardly,' he answered, laying a great stress upon the word.

'I can't understand how they could behave badly to you. But, tell me, what did they do? you never will tell me anything;' and once more she began weeping.

'But you never tell me anything, either,' he said in a low gentle voice.

'Yet you're the most in fault, Arne: I've been so long used to be silent through your father; you ought to have led me on a little. Good Lord! we've only each other; and we've suffered so much together.'

'Well, we must try to manage better,' Arne whispered.

...'Next Sunday I'll read the sermon to you.'

'God bless you for it... Arne!'

'Well?'

'There's something I must tell you.'

'Well, mother, tell me it.'

'I've greatly sinned against you; I've done something very wrong.'

'You, mother?'

'Indeed, I have; but I couldn't help doing it. Arne, you must forgive me.'

'But I'm sure you've never done anything wrong to me.'

'Indeed, I have: and my very love to you made me do it. But you must forgive me; will you?'

'Yes, I will.'

'And then another time I'll tell you all about it... but you must forgive me!'

'Yes, mother, yes.'

'And don't you see the reason why I couldn't talk much to you was, that I had this on my mind? I've sinned against you.'

'Pray don't talk so, mother!'

'Well, I'm glad I've said what I have.'

'And, mother, we'll talk more together, we two.'

'Yes, that we will; and then you'll read the sermon to me?'

'I will.'

'Poor Arne; God bless you!'

'I think we both had better go home now.'

'Yes, we'll both go home.'

'You're looking all round, mother?'

'Yes; your father once lay weeping in this barn.'

'Father?' asked Arne, growing deadly pale.

'Poor Nils! It was the day you were christened.'

'You're looking all round, Arne?'

VIII.

THE SHADOWS ON THE WATER

'It was such a cheerful, sunny day,
No rest indoors could I find;
So I strolled to the wood, and down I lay,
And rocked what came in my mind:
But there the emmets crawled on the ground,
And wasps and gnats were stinging around.

'Won't you go out-doors this fine day, dear?' said mother,
as she sat in the porch, spinning.

It was such a cheerful, sunny day,
No rest indoors could I find;
So I went in the birk, and down I lay,
And sang what came in my mind:
But snakes crept out to bask in the sun —
Snakes five feet long, so away I run.

'In such beautiful weather one may go barefoot,' said
mother, taking off her stockings.

It was such a cheerful, sunny day,
Indoors I could not abide;
So I went in a boat, and down I lay,

And floated away with the tide:
But the sun-beams burned till my nose was sore;
So I turned my boat again to the shore.

'This is, indeed, good weather to dry the hay,' said
mother, putting her rake into a swath.

It was such a cheerful, sunny day,
In the house I could not be;
And so from the heat I climbed away
In the boughs of a shady tree:
But caterpillars dropped on my face,
So down I jumped and ran from the place.

'Well, if the cow doesn't get on to-day, she never will get
on,' said mother, glancing up towards the slope.

It was such a cheerful, sunny day,
Indoors I could not remain:
And so for quiet I rowed away
To the waterfall amain:
But there I drowned while bright was the sky:
If you made this, it cannot be I.

'Only three more such sunny days, and we shall get in all
the hay,' said mother, as she went to make my bed.'

Arne when a child had not cared much for fairy-tales; but
now he began to love them, and they led him to the sagas
and old ballads. He also read sermons and other religious
books; and he was gentle and kind to all around him. But in
his mind arose a strange deep longing: he made no more

songs; but walked often alone, not knowing what was within him.

Many of the places around, which formerly he had not even noticed, now appeared to him wondrously beautiful. At the time he and his schoolfellows had to go to the Clergyman to be prepared for confirmation, they used to play near a lake lying just below the parsonage, and called the Swart-water because it lay deep and dark between the mountains. He now often thought of this place; and one evening he went thither.

He sat down behind a grove close to the parsonage, which was built on a steep hill-side, rising high above till it became a mountain. High mountains rose likewise on the opposite shore, so that broad deep shadows fell upon both sides of the lake, but in the middle ran a stripe of bright silvery water. It was a calm evening near sunset, and not a sound was heard save the tinkling of the cattle-bells from the opposite shore. Arne at first did not look straight before him, but downwards along the lake, where the sun was sprinkling burning red ere it sank to rest. There, at the end, the mountains gave way, and between them lay a long low valley, against which the lake beat; but they seemed to run gradually towards each other, and to hold the valley in a great swing. Houses lay thickly scattered all along, the smoke rose and curled away, the fields lay green and reeking, and boats laden with hay were anchored by the shore. Arne saw many people going to and fro, but he heard no noise. Thence his eye went along the shore towards God's dark wood upon the mountain-sides. Through it, man had made his way, and its course was indicated by a winding stripe of dust. This, Arne's eye followed to opposite where he was sitting: there, the wood ended, the mountains opened, and houses lay scattered all over the valley. They were nearer and looked larger than those in the other valley; and they were red-painted, and their large windows glowed in the sunbeams. The fields and meadows stood in strong light, and the smallest child playing in them was clearly seen; glittering white sands lay dry upon the shore, and some dogs and puppies were running there. But suddenly all became sunless and gloomy: the houses looked dark red, the meadows dull green, the sand greyish white, and the children little clumps: a cloud of mist had risen over the mountains, taking away the sunlight. Arne looked down into the water, and there he found all once more: the fields lay rocking, the wood silently drew near, the houses stood looking down, the doors were open, and children went out and in. Fairy-tales and childish things came rushing into his mind, as little fishes come to a bait, swim away, come once more and play round, and again swim away.

'Let's sit down here till your mother comes; I suppose the Clergyman's lady will have finished sometime or other.' Arne was startled: some one had been sitting a little way behind him.

'If I might but stay this one night more,' said an imploring voice, half smothered by tears: it seemed to be that of a girl not quite grown up.

'Now don't cry any more; it's wrong to cry because you're going home to your mother,' was slowly said by a gentle voice, which was evidently that of a man.

'It's not that, I am crying for.'

'Why, then, are you crying?'

'Because I shall not live any longer with Mathilde.'

This was the name of the Clergyman's only daughter; and Arne remembered that a peasant-girl had been brought up with her.

'Still, that couldn't go on for ever.'

'Well, but only one day more father, dear!' and the girl began sobbing.

'No, it's better we take you home now; perhaps, indeed, it's already too late.'

'Too late! Why too late? did ever anybody hear such a thing?'

'You were born a peasant, and a peasant you shall be; we can't afford to keep a lady.'

'But I might remain a peasant all the same if I stayed there.'

'Of that you can't judge.'

'I've always worn my peasant's dress.'

'Clothes have nothing to do with it.'

'I've spun, and woven, and done cooking.'

'Neither is that the thing.'

'I can speak just as you and mother speak.'

'It's not that either.'

'Well, then, I really don't know what it is,' the girl said, laughing.

'Time will show; but I'm afraid you've already got too many thoughts.'

'Thoughts, thoughts! so you always say; I have no thoughts;' and she wept.

'Ah, you're a wind-mill, that you are.'

'The Clergyman never said that.'

'No; but now I say it.'

'Wind-mill? who ever heard such a thing? I won't be a wind-mill.'

'What will you be then?'

'What will I be? who ever heard of such a thing? nothing, I will be.'

'Well, be nothing, then.'

Now the girl laughed; but after a while she said gravely, 'It's wrong of you to say I'm nothing.'

'Dear me, when you said so yourself!'

'Nay; I won't be nothing.'

'Well, then, be everything.'

Again she laughed; but after a while she said in a sad tone, 'The Clergyman never used to make a fool of me in this way.'

'No; but he did make a fool of you.'

'The Clergyman? well, you've never been so kind to me as he was.'

'No; and if I had I should have spoiled you.'

'Well, sour milk can never become sweet.'

'It may when it is boiled to whey.'

She laughed aloud. 'Here comes your mother.' Then the girl again became grave.

'Such a long-winded woman as that Clergyman's lady, I never met with in all my live-long days,' interposed a sharp quick voice. 'Now, make haste, Baard; get up and push off the boat, or we sha'n't get home to-night. The lady wished me to take care that Eli's feet were kept dry. Dear me, she must attend to that herself! Then she said Eli must take a walk every morning for the sake of her health! Did ever anybody hear such stuff! Well, get up, Baard, and push off the boat; I have to make the dough this evening.'

'The chest hasn't come yet,' he said, without rising.

'But the chest isn't to come; it's to be left there till next Sunday. Well, Eli, get up; take your bundle, and come on. Now, get up, Baard.'

Away she went, followed by the girl.

'Come on, come on!' Arne then heard the same voice say from the shore below.

'Have you looked after the plug in the boat?' Baard asked, still without rising.

'Yes, it's put in;' and then Arne heard her drive it in with a scoop.

'But do get up, Baard; I suppose we're not going to stay here all night? Get up, Baard!'

'I'm waiting for the chest.'

'But bless you, dear, haven't I told you it's to be left there till next Sunday?'

'Here it comes,' Baard said, as the rattling of a cart was heard.

'Why, I said it was to be left till next Sunday.'

'I said we were to take it with us.'

Away went the wife to the cart, and carried the bundle and other small things down into the boat. Then Baard rose, went up, and took down the chest himself.

But a girl with streaming hair, and a straw bonnet came running after the cart: it was the Clergyman's daughter. 'Eli, Eli!' she cried while still at a distance.

'Mathilde, Mathilde,' was answered; and the two girls ran towards each other. They met on the hill, embraced each other and wept. Then Mathilde took out something which she had set down on the grass: it was a bird in a cage.

'You shall have Narrifas,' she said; 'mamma wishes you to have it too; you shall have Narrifas... you really shall — and then you'll think of me — and very often row over to me;' and again they wept much.

'Eli, come, Eli! don't keep standing there!' Arne heard the mother say from the shore below.

'But I'll go with you,' said Mathilde.

'Oh, do, do!' and, with their arms round each other's neck, they ran down to the landing-place.

In a few minutes Arne saw the boat on the water, Eli standing high in the stern, holding the bird-cage, and waving her hand; while Mathilde sat alone on the stones of the landing-place weeping.

She remained sitting there watching the boat as long as it was on the water; and so did Arne. The distance across the lake to the red houses was but short; the boat soon passed into the dark shadows, and he saw it come ashore. Then he saw in the water the reflections of the three who had just landed, and in it he followed them on their way to the red houses till they reached the finest of them; there he saw them go in; the mother first, next, the father, and last, the daughter. But soon the daughter came out again, and seated herself before the storehouse; perhaps to look across to the parsonage, over which the sun was laying its last rays. But Mathilde had already gone, and it was only Arne who was sitting there looking at Eli in the water. 'I wonder whether she sees me,' he thought...

He rose and went away. The sun had set, but the summer night was light and the sky clear blue. The mist from the lake and the valleys rose, and lay along the mountain-sides, but their peaks were left clear, and stood looking over to each other. He went higher: the water lay black and deep below; the distant valley shortened and drew nearer the lake; the mountains came nearer the eye and gathered in clumps; the sky itself was lower; and all things became friendly and familiar.

IX.

THE NUTTING-PARTY

'Fair Venevill bounded on lithesome feet
Her lover to meet.
He sang till it sounded afar away,
"Good-day, good-day,"
While blithesome birds were singing on every blooming
    spray.
On Midsummer-day
There is dancing and play;
But now I know not whether she weaves her wreath or
    nay.

'She wove him a wreath of corn-flowers blue:
"Mine eyes so true."
He took it, but soon away it was flung:
"Farewell!" he sung;
And still with merry singing across the fields he sprung.
On Midsummer-day, &c.

'She wove him a chain: "Oh keep it with care;
'Tis made of my hair."
She yielded him then, in an hour of bliss,
Her pure first kiss;

But he blushed as deeply as she the while her lips met his
On Midsummer-day, &c.

'She wove him a wreath with a lily-band:
"My true right hand."
She wove him another with roses aglow:
"My left hand now."
He took them gently from her, but blushes dyed his brow.
On Midsummer-day, &c.

'She wove him a wreath of all flowers round:
"All I have found."
She wept, but she gathered and wove on still:
"Take all you will."
Without a word he took it, and fled across the hill.
On Midsummer-day, &c.

'She wove on bewildered and out of breath:
"My bridal wreath."
She wove till her fingers aweary had grown:
"Now put it on:"
But when she turned to see him, she found that he had
    gone.
On Midsummer-day, &c.

'She wove on in haste, as for life or death,
Her bridal wreath;
But the Midsummer sun no longer shone,
And the flowers were gone;
But though she had no flowers, wild fancy still wove on.
On Midsummer-day
There is dancing and play;

But now I know not whether she weaves her wreath or
    nay.'

Arne had of late been happier, both when at home and
when out among people. In the winter, when he had not
work enough on his own place, he went out in the parish and
did carpentry; but every Saturday night he came home to the
mother; and went with her to church on Sunday, or read the
sermon to her; and then returned in the evening to his place
of work. But soon, through going more among people, his
wish to travel awoke within him again; and just after his
merriest moods, he would often lie trying to finish his song,
'Over the mountains high,' and altering it for about the
twentieth time. He often thought of Christian, who seemed
to have so utterly forgotten him, and who, in spite of his
promise, had not sent him even a single letter. Once, the
remembrance of Christian came upon him so powerfully that
he thoughtlessly spoke of him to the mother; she gave no
answer, but turned away and went out.

There was living in the parish a jolly man named Ejnar
Aasen. When he was twenty years old he broke his leg, and
from that time he had walked with the support of a stick; but
wherever he appeared limping along on that stick, there was
always merriment going on. The man was rich, and he used
the greater part of his wealth in doing good; but he did it all
so quietly that few people knew anything about it. There was
a large nut-wood on his property; and on one of the brightest
mornings in harvest-time, he always had a nutting-party of
merry girls at his house, where he had abundance of good
cheer for them all day, and a dance in the evening. He was
the godfather of most of the girls; for he was the godfather of

half of the parish. All the children called him Godfather, and from them everybody else had learned to call him so, too.

He and Arne knew each other well; and he liked Arne for the sake of his songs. Now he invited him to the nutting-party; but Arne declined: he was not used to girls' company, he said. 'Then you had better get used to it,' answered Godfather.

So Arne came to the party, and was nearly the only young man among the many girls. Such fun as was there, Arne had never seen before in all his life; and one thing which especially astonished him was, that the girls laughed for nothing at all: if three laughed, then five would laugh just because those three laughed. Altogether, they behaved as if they had lived with each other all their lives; and yet there were several of them who had never met before that very day. When they caught the bough which they jumped after, they laughed, and when they did not catch it they laughed also; when they did not find any nuts, they laughed because they found none; and when they did find some, they also laughed. They fought for the nutting-hook: those who got it laughed, and those who did not get it laughed also. Godfather limped after them, trying to beat them with his stick, and making all the mischief he was good for; those he hit, laughed because he hit them, and those he missed, laughed because he missed them. But the whole lot laughed at Arne because he was so grave; and when at last he could not help laughing, they all laughed again because he laughed.

Then the whole party seated themselves on a large hill; the girls in a circle, and Godfather in the middle. The sun was scorching hot, but they did not care the least for it, but sat cracking nuts, giving Godfather the kernels, and throwing the shells and husks at each other. Godfather "sh "shed at them, and, as far as he could reach, beat them with his stick; for he wanted to make them be quiet and tell tales. But to stop their noise seemed just about as easy as to stop a carriage running down a hill. Godfather began to tell a tale, however. At first many of them would not listen; they knew his stories already; but soon they all listened attentively; and before they thought of it, they set off tale-telling themselves at full gallop. Though they had just been so noisy, their tales, to Arne's great surprise, were very earnest: they ran principally upon love.

'You, Aasa, know a good tale, I remember from last year,' said Godfather, turning to a plump girl with a round, good-natured face, who sat plaiting the hair of a younger sister, whose head lay in her lap.

'But perhaps several know it already,' answered Aasa.

'Never mind, tell it,' they begged.

'Very well, I'll tell it without any more persuading,' she answered; and then, plaiting her sister's hair all the while, she told and sang:

'There was once a grown-up lad who tended cattle, and who often drove them upwards near a broad stream. On one side was a high steep cliff, jutting out so far over the stream that when he was upon it he could talk to any one on the opposite side; and all day he could see a girl over there tending cattle, but he couldn't go to her.

'"Now, tell me thy name, thou girl that art sitting
Up there with thy sheep, so busily knitting,"

'he asked over and over for many days, till one day at last there came an answer:

"'My name floats about like a duck in wet weather;
Come over, thou boy in the cap of brown leather."

'This left the lad no wiser than he was before; and he thought he wouldn't mind her any further. This, however, was much more easily thought than done, for drive his cattle whichever way he would, it always, somehow or other, led to that same high steep cliff. Then the lad grew frightened; and he called over to her:

"'Well, who is your father, and where are you biding?
On the road to the church I have ne'er seen you riding."

'The lad asked this because he half believed she was a *huldre*.*

"'My house is burned down, and my father is drowned,
And the road to the church-hill I never have found."

'This again left the lad no wiser than he was before. In the daytime he kept hovering about the cliff; and at night he dreamed she danced with him, and lashed him with a big cow's tail whenever he tried to catch her. Soon he could neither sleep nor work; and altogether the lad got in a very poor way. Then once more he called from the cliff:

"'If thou art a *huldre*, then pray do not spell me;
If thou art a maiden, then hasten to tell me."

'But there came no answer; and so he was sure she was a *huldre*. He gave up tending cattle; but it was all the same; wherever he went, and whatever he did, he was all the while thinking of the beautiful *huldre* who blew on the horn. Soon he could bear it no longer; and one moonlight evening when all were asleep, he stole away into the forest, which stood there all dark at the bottom, but with its tree-tops bright in the moonbeams. He sat down on the cliff, and called:

"'Run forward, my *huldre*; my love has o'ercome me;
My life is a burden; no longer hide from me."

'The lad looked and looked; but she didn't appear. Then he heard something moving behind him; he turned round and saw a big black bear, which came forward, squatted on the ground and looked at him. But he ran away from the cliff and through the forest as fast as his legs could carry him: if the bear followed him, he didn't know, for he didn't turn round till he lay safely in bed.

"'It was one of her herd," the lad thought; "it isn't worth while to go there any more;" and he didn't go.

'Then, one day, while he was chopping wood, a girl came across the yard who was the living picture of the *huldre*: but when she drew nearer, he saw it wasn't she. Over this he pondered much. Then he saw the girl coming back, and again while she was at a distance she seemed to be the *huldre*, and he ran to meet her; but as soon as he came near, he saw it wasn't she.

'After this, wherever the lad was — at church at dances, or any other parties — the girl was, too; and still when at a distance she seemed to be the *huldre*, and when near she was somebody else. Then he asked her whether she was the *huldre* or not, but she only laughed at him. "One may as well leap into it as creep into it," the lad thought; and so he married the girl.

'But the lad had hardly done this before he ceased to like the girl: when he was away from her he longed for her; but when he was with her he yearned for some one he did not see. So the lad behaved very badly to his wife; but she suffered in silence.

'Then one day when he was out looking for his horses, he came again to the cliff; and he sat down and called out:

"'Like fairy moonlight, to me thou seemest;
Like Midsummer-fires, from afar thou gleamest."

'He felt that it did him good to sit there; and afterwards he went whenever things were wrong at home. His wife wept when he was gone.

'But one day when he was sitting there, he saw the *huldre* sitting all alive on the other side blowing her horn. He called over:

"'Ah, dear, art thou come! all around thee is shining!
Ah, blow now again! I am sitting here pining."

'Then she answered:

"'Away from thy mind the dreams I am blowing;
Thy rye is all rotting for want of mowing."

'But then the lad felt frightened and went home again. Ere long, however, he grew so tired of his wife that he was obliged to go to the forest again, and he sat down on the cliff. Then was sung over to him:

"'I dreamed thou wast here; ho, hasten to bind me!
No; not over there, but behind you will find me."

'The lad jumped up and looked around him, and caught a glimpse of a green petticoat just slipping away between the shrubs. He followed, and it came to a hunting all through the forest. So swift-footed as that *huldre*, no human creature could be: he flung steel over her again and again, but still she ran on just as well as ever. But soon the lad saw, by her pace, that she was beginning to grow tired, though he saw, too, by her shape, that she could be no other than the *huldre*. "Now," he thought, you'll be mine easily;" and he caught hold on her so suddenly and roughly that they both fell, and rolled down the hills a long way before they could stop themselves. Then the *huldre* laughed till it seemed to the lad the mountains sang again. He took her upon his knee; and so beautiful she was, that never in all his life he had seen any one like her: exactly like her, he thought his wife should have been. "Ah, who are you who are so beautiful?" he asked, stroking her cheek. She blushed rosy red. "I'm your wife," she answered.'

The girls laughed much at that tale, and ridiculed the lad. But Godfather asked Arne if he had listened well to it.

'Well, now I'll tell you something,' said a little girl with a little round face, and a very little nose:

'Once there was a little lad who wished very much to woo a little girl. They were both grown up; but yet they were very little. And the lad couldn't in any way muster courage to ask her to have him. He kept close to her when they came home from church; but, somehow or other, their chat was always about the weather. He went over to her at the dancing-parties, and nearly danced her to death; but still he couldn't bring himself to say what he wanted. "You must learn to write," he said to himself; "then you'll manage matters." And the lad set to writing; but he thought it could never be done well enough; and so he wrote a whole year round before he dared do his letter. Now, the thing was to get it given to her without anybody seeing. He waited till one day when they were standing all by themselves behind the church. "I've got a letter for you," said the lad. "But I can't read writing," the girl answered.

'And there the lad stood.

'Then he went to service at the girl's father's house; and he used to keep hovering round her all day long. Once he had nearly brought himself to speak; in fact, he had already opened his mouth; but then a big fly flew in it. "Well, I hope, at any rate, nobody else will come to take her away," the lad thought; but nobody came to take her, because she was so very little.

'By-and-by, however, some one did come, and he, too, was little. The lad could see very well what he wanted; and when he and the girl went up-stairs together, the lad placed himself at the key-hole. Then he who was inside made his offer. "Bad luck to me, I, codfish, who didn't make haste!" the lad thought. He who was inside kissed the girl just on her lips. "No doubt that tasted nice," the lad thought. But he who was inside took the girl on his lap. "Oh, dear me! what a world this is!" the lad said, and began crying. Then the girl heard him and went to the door. "What do you want, you nasty boy?" said she, "why can't you leave me alone?" "I? I only wanted to ask you to have me for your bridesman." "No; that, my brother's going to be," the girl answered, banging the door to.

'And there the lad stood.'

The girls laughed very much at this tale, and afterwards pelted each other with husks.

Then Godfather wished Eli Böen to tell something.

'What, then, must it be?'

'Well, she might tell what she had told him on the hill, the last time he came to see her parents, when she gave him the new garters. Eli laughed very much; and it was some time before she would tell it: however, she did at last:

'A lad and a girl were once walking together on a road. "Ah, look at that thrush that follows us!" the girl said. "It follows me," said the lad. "It's just as likely to be me," the girl answered. "That, we'll soon find out," said the lad; "you go that way, while I go this, and we'll meet up yonder." They did so. "Well, didn't it follow me?" the lad asked, when they met. "No; it followed me," answered the girl. "Then, there must be two." They went together again for some distance, but then there was only one thrush; and the lad thought it flew on his side, but the girl thought it flew on hers. "Devil a bit, I care for that thrush," said the lad. "Nor do I," answered the girl.

'But no sooner had they said this, than the thrush flew away. "It was on your side, it was," said the lad. "Thank you," answered the girl; "but I clearly saw it was on your side. But see! there it comes again!" "Indeed, it's on my side," the lad exclaimed. Then the girl got angry: "Ah, well, I wish I may never stir if I go with you any longer!" and she went away.

'Then the thrush, too, left the lad; and he felt so dull that he called out to the girl, "Is the thrush with you?" "No; isn't it with you?" "Ah, no; you must come here again, and then perhaps it will follow you."

'The girl came; and she and the lad walked on together, hand in hand. "Quitt, quitt, quitt, quitt!" sounded on the girl's side; "quitt, quitt, quitt, quitt!" sounded on the lad's side; "quitt, quitt, quitt, quitt!" sounded on every side;

and when they looked there were a hundred thousand million thrushes all round them. "Ah, how nice this is!" said the girl, looking up at the lad. "Ah, God bless you!" said he, and kissed her.'

All the girls thought this was such a nice tale.

Then Godfather said they must tell what they had dreamed last night, and he would decide who had dreamed the nicest things.

'Tell what they had dreamed! No; impossible!'

And then there was no end of tittering and whispering. But soon one after another began to think she had such a nice dream last night; and then others thought it could not possibly be so nice as what they had dreamed; and at last they all got a great mind for telling their dreams. Yet they must not be told aloud, but to one only, and that one must by no means be Godfather. Arne had all this time been sitting quietly a little lower down the hill, and so the girls thought they dared tell their dreams to him.

Then Arne seated himself under a hazel-bush; and Aasa, the girl who had told the first tale, came over to him. She hesitated a while, but then began:

'I dreamed I was standing by a large lake. Then I saw one walking on the water, and it was one whose name I will not say. He stepped into a large water-lily, and sat there singing. But I launched out upon one of the large leaves of the lily which lay floating on the water; for on it I would row over to him. But no sooner had I come upon the leaf than it began to sink with me, and I became much frightened, and I wept. Then he came rowing along in the water-lily, and lifted me up to him; and we rowed all over the whole lake. Wasn't that a nice dream?'

Next came the little girl who had told the tale about the little lad:

'I dreamed I had caught a little bird, and I was so pleased with it, and I thought I wouldn't let it loose till I came home in our room. But there I dared not let it loose, for I was afraid father and mother might tell me to let it go again. So I took it up-stairs; but I could not let it loose there, either, for the cat was lurking about. Then I didn't know what in the world to do; yet I took it into the barn. Dear me, there were so many cracks, I was afraid it might go away! Well, then I went down again into the yard; and there, it seemed to me some one was standing whose name I will not say. He stood playing with a big, big dog. "I would rather play with that bird of yours," he said, and drew very near to me. But then it seemed to me I began running away; and both he and the big dog ran after me all round the yard; but then mother opened the front door, pulled me hastily in, and banged the door after me. The lad, however, stood laughing outside, with his face against the window-pane. "Look, here's the bird," he said; and, only think, he had my bird out there! Wasn't that a beautiful dream?'

Then came the girl who had told about the thrushes — Eli, they called her. She was laughing so much that she could not speak for some time; but at last she began:

'I had been looking forward with very much pleasure to our nutting in the wood to-day; and so last night I dreamed I was sitting here on the hill. The sun shone brightly; and I had my lap full of nuts. But there came a little squirrel among them, and it sat on its hind-legs and ate them all up. Wasn't that a funny dream?'

Afterwards some more dreams were told him; and then the girls would have him say which was the nicest. Of course, he must have plenty of time for consideration; and meanwhile Godfather and the whole flock went down to the house, leaving Arne to follow. They skipped down the hill, and when they came to the plain went all in a row singing towards the house.

Arne sat alone on the hill, listening to the singing. Strong sunlight fell on the group of girls, and their white bodices shone bright, as they went dancing over the meadows, every now and then clasping each other round the waist; while Godfather limped behind, threatening them with a stick because they trod down his hay. Arne thought no more of the dreams, and soon he no longer looked after the girls. His thoughts went floating far away beyond the valley, like the fine air-threads, while he remained behind on the hill, spinning; and before he was aware of it he had woven a close web of sadness. More than ever, he longed to go away.

'Why stay any longer?' he said to himself; 'surely, I've been lingering long enough now!' He promised himself that he would speak to the mother about it as soon as he reached home, however it might turn out.

With greater force than ever, his thoughts turned to his song, 'Over the mountains high;' and never before had the words come so swiftly, or linked themselves into rhyme so easily; they seemed almost like girls sitting in a circle on the brow of a hill. He had a piece of paper with him, and placing it upon his knee, he wrote down the verses as they came. When he had finished the song, he rose like one freed from a burden. He felt unwilling to see any one, and went homewards by the way through the wood, though he knew he should then have to walk during the night. The first time he stopped to rest on the way, he put his hand to his pocket to take out the song, intending to sing it aloud to himself through the wood; but he found he had left it behind at the place where it was composed.

One of the girls went on the hill to look for him; she did not find him, but she found his song.

X.

LOOSENING THE WEATHER-VANE

To speak to the mother about going away, was more easily thought of than done. He spoke again about Christian, and those letters which had never come; but then the mother went away, and for days afterwards he thought her eyes looked red and swollen. He noticed, too, that she then got nicer food for him than usual; and this gave him another sign of her state of mind with regard to him.

One day he went to cut fagots in a wood which bordered upon another belonging to the parsonage, and through which the road ran. Just where he was going to cut his fagots, people used to come in autumn to gather whortleberries. He had laid aside his axe to take off his jacket, and was just going to begin work, when two girls came walking along with a basket to gather berries. He used generally to hide himself rather than meet girls, and he did so now.

'Ah! only see what a lot of berries! Eli, Eli!'

'Yes, dear, I see!'

'Well, but, then, don't go any farther; here are many basketfuls.'

'I thought I heard a rustling among the trees!'

'Oh, nonsense!'

The girls rushed towards each other, clasped each other round the waist, and for a little while stood still, scarcely drawing breath. 'It's nothing, I dare say; come, let's go on picking.'

'Well, so we will.'

And they went on.

'It was nice you came to the parsonage to-day, Eli. Haven't you anything to tell me?'

'Yes; I've been to see Godfather.'

'Well, you've told me that; but haven't you anything to tell me about him — you know who?'

'Yes, indeed I have!'

'Oh! Eli, have you! make haste and tell me!' 'He has been there again.'

'Nonsense?'

'Indeed, he has: father and mother pretended to know nothing of it; but I went up-stairs and hid myself.'

'Well, what then? did he come after you?'

'Yes; I believe father told him where I was; he's always so tiresome now.'

'And so he came there? — Sit down, sit down; here, near me. Well, and then he came?'

'Yes; but he didn't say much, for he was so bashful.'

'Tell me what he said, every word; pray, every word!'

'"Are you afraid of me?" he said. "Why should I be afraid?" I answered. "You know what I want to say to you," he said, sitting down beside me on the chest.'

'Beside you!'

'And he took me round my waist.'

'Round your waist; nonsense!'

'I wished very much to get loose again; but he wouldn't let me. "Dear Eli," he said—' She laughed, and the other one laughed, too.

'Well? well?'

'"Will you be my wife?" Ha, ha, ha!'

'Ha, ha, ha!'

And then both laughed together, 'Ha, ha, ha, ha!'

At last the laughing came to an end, and they were both quiet for a while. Then the one who had first spoken asked in a low voice, 'Wasn't it strange he took you round your waist?'

Either the other girl did not answer that question, or she answered in so low a voice that it could not be heard; perhaps she only answered by a smile.

'Didn't your father or your mother say anything afterwards?' asked the first girl, after a pause.

'Father came up and looked at me; but I turned away from him because he laughed at me.'

'And your mother?'

'No, she didn't say anything; but she wasn't so strict as usual.'

'Well, you've done with him, I think?'

'Of course!'

Then there was again silence awhile.

'Was it thus he took you round your waist?'

'No; thus.'

'Well, then — it was thus...'

'Eli?'

'Well?'

'Do you think there will ever be anybody come in that way to me?'

'Of course, there will!'

'Nonsense! Ah, Eli? If he took me round the waist?' She hid her face.

Then they laughed again; and there was much whispering and tittering.

Soon the girls went away; they had not seen either Arne or the axe and jacket, and he was glad of it.

A few days after, he gave Opplands-Knut a little farm on Kampen. 'You shall not be lonely any longer,' Arne said.

That winter Arne went to the parsonage for some time to do carpentry; and both the girls were often there together. When Arne saw them, he often wondered who it might be that now came to woo Eli Böen.

One day he had to drive for the clergyman's daughter and Eli; he could not understand a word they said, though he had very quick ears. Sometimes Mathilde spoke to him; and then Eli always laughed and hid her face. Mathilde asked him if it was true that he could make verses. 'No,' he said quickly; then they both laughed; and chattered and laughed again. He felt vexed; and afterwards when he met them seemed not to take any notice of them.

Once he was sitting in the servants" hall while a dance was going on, and Mathilde and Eli both came to see it. They stood together in a corner, disputing about something; Eli would not do it, but Mathilde would, and she at last gained her point. Then they both came over to Arne, courtesied, and asked him if he could dance. He said he could not; and then both turned aside and ran away, laughing. In fact, they were always laughing, Arne thought; and he became brave. But soon after, he got the clergyman's foster-son, a boy of about twelve, to teach him to dance, when no one was by.

Eli had a little brother of the same age as the clergyman's foster-son. These two boys were playfellows; and Arne made sledges, snow-shoes and snares for them; and often talked to them about their sisters, especially about Eli. One day Eli's brother brought Arne a message that he ought to make his hair a little smoother. 'Who said that?'

'Eli did; but she told me not to say it was she.'

A few days after, Arne sent word that Eli ought to laugh a little less. The boy brought back word that Arne ought by all means to laugh a little more.

Eli's brother once asked Arne to give him something that he had written. He complied, without thinking any more about the matter. But in a few days after, the boy, thinking to please Arne, told him that Eli and Mathilde liked his writing very much.

'Where, then, have they seen any of it?'

'Well, it was for them, I asked for some of it the other day.'

Then Arne asked the boys to bring him something their sisters had written. They did so; and he corrected the errors in the writing with his carpenter's pencil, and asked the boys to lay it in some place where their sisters might easily find it. Soon after, he found the paper in his jacket pocket; and at the foot was written, 'Corrected by a conceited fellow.'

The next day, Arne completed his work at the parsonage, and returned home. So gentle as he was that winter, the mother had never seen him, since that sad time just after the father's death. He read the sermon to her, accompanied her to church, and was in every way very kind. But she knew only too well that one great reason for his increased kindness was, that he meant to go away when spring came. Then one day a message came from Böen, asking him to go there to do carpentry.

Arne started, and, apparently without thinking of what he said, replied that he would come. But no sooner had the messenger left than the mother said, 'You may well be astonished! From Böen?'

'Well, is there anything strange in that?' Arne asked, without looking at her.

'From Böen!' the mother exclaimed once more.

'And, why not from Böen, as well as any other place?' he answered, looking up a little.

'From Böen and Birgit Böen! — Baard, who made your father a cripple, and all only for Birgit's sake!'

'What do you say?' exclaimed Arne; 'was that Baard Böen?'

Mother and son stood looking at each other. The whole of the father's life seemed unrolled before them, and at that moment they saw the black thread which had always run through it. Then they began talking about those grand days of his, when old Eli Böen had himself offered him his daughter Birgit, and he had refused her: they passed on through his life till the day when his spine had been broken; and they both agreed that Baard's fault was the less. Still, it was he who had made the father a cripple; he, it was.

'Have I not even yet done with father?' Arne thought; and determined at the same moment that he would go to Böen.

As he went walking, with his saw on his shoulder, over the ice towards Böen, it seemed to him a beautiful place. The dwelling-house always seemed as if it was fresh painted; and — perhaps because he felt a little cold — it just then looked to him very sheltered and comfortable. He did not, however, go straight in, but went round by the cattle-house, where a flock of thick-haired goats stood in the snow, gnawing the bark off some fir twigs. A shepherd's dog ran backwards and forwards on the barn steps, barking as if the devil was coming to the house; but when Arne went to him, he wagged his tail and allowed himself to be patted. The kitchen door at the upper end of the house was often opened, and Arne looked over there every time; but he saw no one except the milkmaid, carrying some pails, or the cook, throwing something to the goats. In the barn the threshers were hard at work; and to the left, in front of the woodshed, a lad stood chopping fagots, with many piles of them behind him.

Arne laid away his saw and went into the kitchen: the floor was strewed with white sand and chopped juniper leaves; copper kettles shone on the walls; china and earthenware stood in rows upon the shelves; and the servants were preparing the dinner. Arne asked for Baard. 'Step into the sitting-room,' said one of the servants, pointing to an inner door with a brass knob. He went in: the room was brightly painted — the ceiling, with clusters of roses; the cupboards, with red, and the names of the owners in black letters; the bedstead, also with red, bordered with blue stripes. Beside the stove, a broad-shouldered, mild-looking man, with long light hair, sat hooping some tubs; and at the large table, a slender, tall woman, in a close-fitting dress and linen cap, sat sorting some corn into two heaps: no one else was in the room.

'Good day, and a blessing on the work,' said Arne, taking off his cap. Both looked up; and the man smiled and asked who it was. 'I am he who has come to do carpentry.'

The man smiled still more, and said, while he leaned forward again to his work, 'Oh, all right, Arne Kampen.'

'Arne Kampen?' exclaimed the wife, staring down at the floor. The man looked up quickly, and said, smiling once more, 'A son of Nils, the tailor;' and then he began working again.

Soon the wife rose, went to the shelf, turned from it to the cupboard, once more turned away, and, while rummaging for something in the table drawer, she asked, without looking up, 'Is he going to work here?'

'Yes, that he is,' the husband answered, also without looking up.

'Nobody has asked you to sit down, it seems,' he added, turning to Arne, who then took a seat. The wife went out, and the husband continued working: and so Arne asked whether he, too, might begin. 'We'll have dinner first.'

The wife did not return; but next time the door opened, it was Eli who entered. At first, she appeared not to see Arne, but when he rose to meet her she turned half round and gave him her hand; yet she did not look at him. They exchanged a few words, while the father worked on. Eli was slender and upright, her hands were small, with round wrists, her hair was braided, and she wore a dress with a close-fitting bodice. She laid the table for dinner: the labourers dined in the next room; but Arne, with the family.

'Isn't your mother coming?' asked the husband.

'No; she's up-stairs, weighing wool.'

'Have you asked her to come?'

'Yes; but she says she won't have anything.'

There was silence for a while.

'But it's cold up-stairs.'

'She wouldn't let me make a fire.'

After dinner, Arne began to work; and in the evening he again sat with the family. The wife and Eli sewed, while the husband employed himself in some trifling work, and Arne helped him. They worked on in silence above an hour; for Eli, who seemed to be the one who usually did the talking, now said nothing. Arne thought with dismay how often it was just so in his own home; and yet he had never felt it till now. At last, Eli seemed to think she had been silent quite long enough, and, after drawing a deep breath, she burst out laughing. Then the father laughed; and Arne felt it was ridiculous and began, too. Afterwards they talked about several things, soon the conversation was principally between Arne and Eli, the father now and then putting in a word edgewise. But once after Arne had been speaking at some length, he looked up, and his eyes met those of the mother, Birgit, who had laid down her work, and sat gazing at him. Then she went on with her work again; but the next word he spoke made her look up once more.

Bedtime drew near, and they all went to their own rooms. Arne thought he would take notice of the dream he had the first night in a fresh place; but he could see no meaning in it. During the whole day he had talked very little with the husband; yet now in the night he dreamed of no one in the house but him. The last thing was, that Baard was sitting playing at cards with Nils, the tailor. The latter looked very pale and angry; but Baard was smiling, and he took all the tricks.

Arne stayed at Böen several days; and a great deal was done, but very little said. Not only the people in the parlor, but also the servants, the housemen, everybody about the place, even the women, were silent. In the yard was an old dog which barked whenever a stranger came near; but if any of the people belonging to the place heard him, they always said 'Hush!' and then he went away, growling, and lay down. At Arne's own home was a large weather-vane, and here was one still larger which he particularly noticed because it did not turn. It shook whenever the wind was high, as though it wished to turn; and Arne stood looking at it so long that he felt at last he must climb up to unloose it. It was not frozen fast, as he thought: but a stick was fixed against it to prevent it from turning. He took the stick out and threw it down; Baard was just passing below, and it struck him.

'What are you doing?' said he, looking up.

'I'm loosening the vane.'

'Leave it alone; it makes a wailing noise when it turns.'

'Well, I think even that's better than silence,' said Arne, seating himself astride on the ridge of the roof. Baard looked up at Arne, and Arne down at Baard. Then Baard smiled and said, 'He who must wail when he speaks had better he silent.'

Words sometimes haunt us long after they were uttered, especially when they were last words. So Baard's words followed Arne as he came down from the roof in the cold, and they were still with him when he went into the sitting-room in the evening. It was twilight; and Eli stood at the window, looking away over the ice which lay bright in the moonlight. Arne went to the other window, and looked out also. Indoors it was warm and quiet; outdoors it was cold, and a sharp wind swept through the vale, bending the branches of the trees, and making their shadows creep trembling on the snow. A light shone over from the parsonage, then vanished, then appeared again, taking various shapes and colours, as a distant light always seems to do when one looks at it long and intently. Opposite, the mountain stood dark, with deep shadow at its foot, where a thousand fairy tales hovered; but with its snowy upper plains bright in the moonlight. The stars were shining, and northern lights were flickering in one quarter of the sky, but they did not spread. A little way from the window, down towards the water, stood some trees, whose shadows kept stealing over to each other; but the tall ash stood alone, writing on the snow.

All was silent, save now and then, when a long wailing sound was heard. 'What's that?' asked Arne.

'It's the weather-vane,' said Eli; and after a little while she added in a lower tone, as if to herself, 'it must have come unfastened.'

But Arne had been like one who wished to speak and could not. Now he said, 'Do you remember that tale about the thrushes?'

'Yes.'

'It was you who told it, indeed. It was a nice tale.'

'I often think there's something that sings when all is still,' she said, in a voice so soft and low that he felt as if he heard it now for the first time.

'It is the good within our own souls,' he said.

She looked at him as if she thought that answer meant too much; and they both stood silent a few moments. Then she asked, while she wrote with her finger on the window-pane, 'Have you made any songs lately?'

He blushed; but she did not see it, and so she asked once more, 'How do you manage to make songs?'

'Should you like to know?'

'Well, yes — I should.'

'I store up the thoughts that other people let slip.'

She was silent for a long while; perhaps thinking she might have had some thoughts fit for songs, but had let them slip.

'How strange it is,' she said, at last, as though to herself, and beginning to write again on the window-pane.

'I made a song the first time I had seen you.'

'Where was that?'

'Behind the parsonage, that evening you went away from there — I saw you in the water.'

She laughed, and was quiet for a while.

'Let me hear that song.'

Arne had never done such a thing before, but he repeated the song now:

'Fair Venevill bounded on lithesome feet
Her lover to meet,' &c.*

Eli listened attentively, and stood silent long after he had finished. At last she exclaimed, 'Ah, what a pity for her!'

'I feel as if I had not made that song myself,' he said; and then stood like her, thinking over it.

'But that won't be my fate, I hope,' she said, after a pause.

'No; I was thinking rather of myself.'

'Will it be your fate, then?'

'I don't know; I felt so then.'

'How strange.' She wrote on the panes again.

The next day, when Arne came into the room to dinner, he went over to the window. Outdoors it was dull and foggy, but indoors, warm and comfortable; and on the window-pane was written with a finger, 'Arne, Arne, Arne,' and nothing but

'Arne,' over and over again: it was at that window, Eli stood
the evening before.

XI.
ELI'S SICKNESS

Next day, Arne came into the room and said he had heard in the yard that the clergyman's daughter, Mathilde, had just gone to the town; as she thought, for a few days, but as her parents intended, for a year or two. Eli had heard nothing of this before, and now she fell down fainting. Arne had never seen any one faint, and he was much frightened. He ran for the maids; they ran for the parents, who came hurrying in; and there was a disturbance all over the house, and the dog barked on the barn steps. Soon after, when Arne came in again, the mother was kneeling at the bedside, while the father supported Eli's drooping head. The maids were running about — one for water, another for hartshorn which was in the cupboard, while a third unfastened her jacket.

'God help you!' the mother said; 'I see it was wrong in us not to tell her; it was you, Baard, who would have it so; God help you!' Baard did not answer. 'I wished to tell her, indeed; but nothing's to be as I wish; God help you! You're always so harsh with her, Baard; you don't understand her; you don't know what it is to love anybody, you don't.' Baard did not answer. 'She isn't like some others who can bear sorrow; it quite puts her down, poor slight thing, as she is. Wake up, my child, and we'll be kind to you! wake up, Eli, my own darling, and don't grieve us so.'

'You always either talk too much or too little,' Baard said, at last, looking over to Arne, as though he did not wish him to hear such things, but to leave the room. As, however, the maid-servants stayed, Arne thought he, too, might stay; but he went over to the window. Soon the sick girl revived so far as to be able to look round and recognize those about her; but then also memory returned, and she called wildly for Mathilde, went into hysterics, and sobbed till it was painful to be in the room. The mother tried to soothe her, and the father sat down where she could see him; but she pushed them both from her.

'Go away!' she cried; 'I don't like you; go away!'

'Oh, Eli, how can you say you don't like your own parents?' exclaimed the mother.

'No! you're unkind to me, and you take away every pleasure from me!'

'Eli, Eli! don't say such hard things,' said the mother, imploringly.

'Yes, mother,' she exclaimed; 'now I must say it! Yes, mother; you wish to marry me to that bad man; and I won't have him! You shut me up here, where I'm never happy save when I'm going out! And you take away Mathilde from me; the only one in the world I love and long for! Oh, God, what will become of me, now Mathilde is gone!'

'But you haven't been much with her lately,' Baard said.

'What did that matter, so long as I could look over to her from that window,' the poor girl answered, weeping in a childlike way that Arne had never before seen in any one.

'Why, you couldn't see her there,' said Baard.

'Still, I saw the house,' she answered; and the mother added passionately, 'You don't understand such things, you don't.' Then Baard said nothing more.

'Now, I can never again go to the window,' said Eli. 'When I rose in the morning, I went there; in the evening I sat there in the moonlight: I went there when I could go to no one else. Mathilde! Mathilde?' She writhed in the bed, and went again into hysterics. Baard sat down on a stool a little way from the bed, and continued looking at her.

But Eli did not recover so soon as they expected. Towards evening they saw she would have a serious illness, which had probably been coming upon her for some time; and Arne was called to assist in carrying her up-stairs to her room. She lay quiet and unconscious, looking very pale. The mother sat by the side of her bed, the father stood at the foot, looking at her: afterwards he went to his work. So did Arne; but that night before he went to sleep, he prayed for her; prayed that she who was so young and fair might be happy in this world, and that no one might bar away joy from her.

The next day when Arne came in, he found the father and mother sitting talking together: the mother had been weeping. Arne asked how Eli was; both expected the other to give an answer, and so for some time none was given, but at last the father said, 'Well, she's very bad to-day.'

Afterwards Arne heard that she had been raving all night, or, as the father said, 'talking foolery.' She had a violent fever, knew no one, and would not eat, and the parents were deliberating whether they should send for a doctor. When afterwards they both went to the sick-room, leaving Arne behind, he felt as if life and death were struggling together up there, but he was kept outside.

In a few days, however, Eli became a little better. But once when the father was tending her, she took it into her head to have Narrifas, the bird which Mathilde had given her, set beside the bed. Then Baard told her that — as was really the case — in the confusion the bird had been forgotten, and was starved. The mother was just coming in as Baard was saying this, and while yet standing in the doorway, she cried out, 'Oh, dear me, what a monster you are, Baard, to tell it to that poor little thing! See, she's fainting again; God forgive you!' When Eli revived she again asked for the bird; said its death was a bad omen for Mathilde; and wished to go to her: then she fainted again. Baard stood looking on till she grew so much worse that he wanted to help, too, in tending her; but the mother pushed him away, and said she would do all herself. Then Baard gave a long sad look at both of them, put his cap straight with both hands, turned aside and went out.

Soon after, the Clergyman and his wife came; for the fever heightened, and grew so violent that they did not know whether it would turn to life or death. The Clergyman as well as his wife spoke to Baard about Eli, and hinted that he was too harsh with her; but when they heard what he had told her about the bird, the Clergyman plainly told him it was very rough, and said he would have her taken to his own house as soon as she was well enough to be moved. The Clergyman's wife would scarcely look at Baard; she wept, and went to sit with the sick one; then sent for the doctor, and came several times a day to carry out his directions. Baard went wandering restlessly about from one place to another in the yard, going oftenest to those places where he could be alone. There he would stand still by the hour together; then, put his cap straight and work again a little.

The mother did not speak to him, and they scarcely looked at each other. He used to go and see Eli several times in the day; he took off his shoes before he went up-stairs, left his cap outside, and opened the door cautiously. When he came in, Birgit would turn her head, but take no notice of him, and then sit just as before, stooping forwards, with her head on her hands, looking at Eli, who lay still and pale, unconscious of all that was passing around her. Baard would stand awhile at the foot of the bed and look at them both, but say nothing: once when Eli moved as though she were waking, he stole away directly as quietly as he had come.

Arne often thought words had been exchanged between man and wife and parents and child which had been long gathering, and would be long remembered. He longed to go away, though he wished to know before he went what would be the end of Eli's illness; but then he thought he might always hear about her even after he had left; and so he went to Baard telling him he wished to go home: the work which he came to do was completed. Baard was sitting outdoors on a chopping-block, scratching in the snow with a stick: Arne recognized the stick: it was the one which had fastened the weather-vane.

'Well, perhaps it isn't worth your while to stay here now; yet I feel as if I don't like you to go away, either,' said Baard, without looking up. He said no more; neither did Arne; but after a while he walked away to do some work, taking for granted that he was to remain at Böen.

Some time after, when he was called to dinner, he saw Baard still sitting on the block. He went over to him, and asked how Eli was.

'I think she's very bad to-day,' Baard said.

'I see the mother's weeping.'

Arne felt as if somebody asked him to sit down, and he seated himself opposite Baard on the end of a felled tree.

'I've often thought of your father lately,' Baard said so unexpectedly that Arne did not know how to answer.

'You know, I suppose, what was between us?'

'Yes, I know.'

'Well, you know, as may be expected, only one half of the story, and think I'm greatly to blame.'

'You have, I dare say, settled that affair with your God, as surely as my father has done so,' Arne said, after a pause.

'Well, some people might think so,' Baard answered. 'When I found this stick, I felt it was so strange that you should come here and unloose the weather-vane. As well now as later, I thought.' He had taken off his cap, and sat silently looking at it.

'I was about fourteen years old when I became acquainted with your father, and he was of the same age. He was very wild, and he couldn't bear any one to be above him in anything. So he always had a grudge against me because I stood first, and he, second, when we were confirmed. He often offered to fight me, but we never came to it; most likely because neither of us felt sure who would beat. And a strange thing it is, that although he fought every day, no accident came from it; while the first time I did, it turned out as badly as could be; but, it's true, I had been wanting to fight long enough.

'Nils fluttered about all the girls, and they, about him. There was only one I would have, and her he took away from me at every dance, at every wedding, and at every party; it was she who is now my wife... Often, as I sat there, I felt a great mind to try my strength upon him for this thing; but I was afraid I should lose, and I knew if I did, I should lose her, too. Then, when everybody had gone, I would lift the weights he had lifted, and kick the beam he had kicked; but the next time he took the girl from me, I was afraid to meddle with him, although once, when he was flirting with her just in my face, I went up to a tall fellow who stood by and threw him against the beam, as if in fun. And Nils grew pale, too, when he saw it.

'Even if he had been kind to her; but he was false to her again and again. I almost believe, too, she loved him all the more every time. Then the last thing happened. I thought now it must either break or bear. The Lord, too, would not have him going about any longer; and so he fell a little more heavily than I meant him to do. I never saw him afterwards.'

They sat silent for a while; then Baard went on:

'I once more made my offer. She said neither yes nor no; but I thought she would like me better afterwards. So we were married. The wedding was kept down in the valley, at the house of one of her aunts, whose property she inherited. We had plenty when we started, and it has now increased. Our estates lay side by side, and when we married they were thrown into one, as I always, from a boy, thought they might be. But many other things didn't turn out as I expected.' He was silent for several minutes; and Arne thought he wept; but he did not.

'In the beginning of our married life, she was quiet and very sad. I had nothing to say to comfort her, and so I was silent. Afterwards, she began sometimes to take to these fidgeting ways which you have, I dare say, noticed in her; yet it was a change, and so I said nothing then, either. But one really happy day, I haven't known ever since I was married, and that's now twenty years...'

He broke the stick in two pieces; and then sat for a while looking at them.

'When Eli grew bigger, I thought she would be happier among strangers than at home. It was seldom I wished to carry out my own will in anything, and whenever I did, it generally turned out badly; so it was in this case. The mother longed after her child, though only the lake lay between them; and afterwards I saw, too, that Eli's training at the parsonage was in some ways not the right thing for her; but then it was too late: now I think she likes neither father nor mother.'

He had taken off his cap again; and now his long hair hung down over his eyes; he stroked it back with both hands, and put on his cap as if he were going away; but when, as he was about to rise, he turned towards the house, he checked himself and added, while looking up at the bed-room window.

'I thought it better that she and Mathilde shouldn't see each other to say good-bye: that, too, was wrong. I told her the wee bird was dead; for it was my fault, and so I thought it better to confess; but that again was wrong. And so it is with everything: I've always meant to do for the best, but it has always turned out for the worst; and now things have come to such a pass that both wife and daughter speak ill of me, and I'm going here lonely.'

A servant-girl called out to them that the dinner was becoming cold. Baard rose. 'I hear the horses neighing; I think somebody has forgotten them,' he said, and went away to the stable to give them some hay.

Arne rose, too; he felt as if he hardly knew whether Baard had been speaking or not.

XII.

A GLIMPSE OF SPRING

Eli felt very weak after the illness. The mother watched by her night and day, and never came down-stairs; the father came up as usual, with his boots off, and leaving his cap outside the door. Arne still remained at the house. He and the father used to sit together in the evening; and Arne began to like him much, for Baard was a well-informed, deep-thinking man, though he seemed afraid of saying what he knew. In his own way, he, too, enjoyed Arne's company, for Arne helped his thoughts and told him of things which were new to him.

Eli soon began to sit up part of the day, and as she recovered, she often took little fancies into her head. Thus, one evening when Arne was sitting in the room below, singing songs in a clear, loud voice, the mother came down with a message from Eli, asking him if he would go up-stairs and sing to her, that she might also hear the words. It seemed as if he had been singing to Eli all the time, for when the mother spoke he turned red, and rose as if he would deny having done so, though no one charged him with it. He soon collected himself, however, and replied evasively, that he could sing so very little. The mother said it did not seem so when he was alone.

Arne yielded and went. He had not seen Eli since the day he helped to carry her up-stairs; he thought she must be much altered, and he felt half afraid to see her. But when he gently opened the door and went in, he found the room quite dark, and he could see no one. He stopped at the door-way.

'Who is it?' Eli asked in a clear, low voice.

'It's Arne Kampen,' he said in a gentle, guarded tone, so that his words might fall softly.

'It was very kind of you to come.'

'How are you, Eli?'

'Thanks, I'm much better now.'

'Won't you sit down, Arne?' she added after a while, and Arne felt his way to a chair at the foot of the bed. 'It did me good to hear you singing; won't you sing a little to me up here?'

'If I only knew anything you would like.'

She was silent a while: then she said, 'Sing a hymn.' And he sang one: it was the confirmation hymn. When he had finished he heard her weeping, and so he was afraid to sing again; but in a little while she said, 'Sing one more.' And he sang another: it was the one which is generally sung while the catechumens are standing in the aisle.

'How many things I've thought over while I've been lying here,' Eli said. He did not know what to answer; and he heard her weeping again in the dark. A clock that was ticking on the wall warned for striking, and then struck. Eli breathed deeply several times, as if she would lighten her breast, and then she said, 'One knows so little; I knew neither father nor mother. I haven't been kind to them; and now it seems so sad to hear that hymn.'

When we talk in the darkness, we speak more faithfully than when we see each other's face; and we also say more.

'It does one good to hear you talk so,' Arne replied, just remembering what she had said when she was taken ill.

She understood what he meant. 'If now this had not happened to me,' she went on, 'God only knows how long I might have gone before I found mother.'

'She has talked matters over with you lately, then?'

'Yes, every day; she has done hardly anything else.'

'Then, I'm sure you've heard many things.'

'You may well say so.'

'I think she spoke of my father?'

'Yes.'

'She remembers him still?'

'She remembers him.'

'He wasn't kind to her.'

'Poor mother!'

'Yet he was worst to himself.'

They were silent; and Arne had thoughts which he could not utter. Eli was the first to link their words again.

'You are said to be like your father.'

'People say so,' he replied evasively.

She did not notice the tone of his voice, and so, after a while she returned to the subject. 'Could he, too, make songs?'

'No.'

'Sing a song to me... one that you've made yourself.'

'I have none,' he said; for it was not his custom to confess he had himself composed the songs he sang.

'I'm sure you have; and I'm sure, too, you'll sing one of them when I ask you.'

What he had never done for any one else, he now did for her, as he sang the following song:

'The Tree's early leaf-buds were bursting their brown:
"Shall I take them away?" said the Frost, sweeping down.
"No; leave them alone
Till the blossoms have grown,"
Prayed the tree, while he trembled from rootlet to crown.

'The Tree bore his blossoms, and all the birds sung:
"Shall I take them away?" said the Wind, as he swung.
"No; leave them alone
Till the berries have grown,"
Said the Tree, while his leaflets quivering hung.

'The Tree bore his fruit in the Midsummer glow:
Said the girl, "May I gather thy berries or no?"
"Yes; all thou canst see;
Take them; all are for thee,"
Said the Tree, while he bent down his laden boughs low.'

That song nearly took her breath away. He, too, remained silent after it, as though he had sung more than he could say.

Darkness has a strong influence over those who are sitting in it and dare not speak: they are never so near each other as then. If she only turned on the pillow, or moved her hand on the blanket, or breathed a little more heavily, he heard it.

'Arne, couldn't you teach me to make songs?'

'Did you never try?'

'Yes, I have, these last few days; but I can't manage it.'

'What, then, did you wish to have in them?'

'Something about my mother, who loved your father so dearly.'

'That's a sad subject.'

'Yes, indeed it is; and I have wept over it.'

'You shouldn't search for subjects; they come of themselves.'

'How do they come?'

'Just as other dear things come — unexpectedly.'

They were both silent. 'I wonder, Arne, you're longing to go away; you who have such a world of beauty within yourself.'

'Do you know I am longing?'

She did not answer, but lay still a few moments as if in thought.

'Arne, you mustn't go away,' she said; and the words came warm to his heart.

'Well, sometimes I have less mind to go.'

'Your mother must love you much, I'm sure. I must see your mother.'

'Go over to Kampen, when you're well again.'

And all at once, he fancied her sitting in the bright room at Kampen, looking out on the mountains; his chest began to heave, and the blood rushed to his face.

'It's warm in here,' he said, rising.

She heard him rise. 'Are you going, Arne?' He sat down again.

'You must come over to see us oftener; mother's so fond of you.'

'I should like to come myself, too... but still I must have some errand.'

Eli lay silent for a while, as if she was turning over something in her mind. 'I believe,' she said, 'mother has something to ask you about...'

They both felt the room was becoming very hot; he wiped his brow, and he heard her rise in the bed. No sound could be heard either in the room or down-stairs, save the ticking of the clock on the wall. There was no moon, and the darkness was deep; when he looked through the green window, it seemed to him as if he was looking into a wood; when he looked towards Eli he could see nothing, but his thoughts went over to her, and then his heart throbbed till he could himself hear its beating. Before his eyes flickered bright sparks; in his ears came a rushing sound; still faster throbbed his heart: he felt he must rise or say something. But then she exclaimed,

'How I wish it were summer!'

'That it were summer?' And he heard again the sound of the cattle-bells, the horn from the mountains, and the singing from the valleys; and saw the fresh green foliage, the Swart-water glittering in the sunbeams, the houses rocking in it, and Eli coming out and sitting on the shore, just as she did that evening. 'If it were summer,' she said, 'and I were sitting on the hill, I think I could sing a song.'

He smiled gladly, and asked, 'What would it be about?'

'About something bright; about — well, I hardly know what myself...'

'Tell me, Eli!' He rose in glad excitement; but, on second thoughts, sat down again.

'No; not for all the world!' she said, laughing.

'I sang to you when you asked me.'

'Yes, I know you did; but I can't tell you this; no! no!'

'Eli, do you think I would laugh at the little verse you have made?'

'No, I don't think you would, Arne; but it isn't anything I've made myself.'

'Oh, it's by somebody else then?'

'Yes.'

'Then, you can surely say it to me.'

'No, no, I can't; don't ask me again, Arne!'

The last words were almost inaudible; it seemed as if she had hidden her head under the bedclothes.

'Eli, now you're not kind to me as I was to you,' he said, rising.

'But, Arne, there's a difference... you don't understand me... but it was... I don't know... another time... don't be offended with me, Arne! don't go away from me!' She began to weep.

'Eli, what's the matter?' It came over him like sunshine. 'Are you ill?' Though he asked, he did not believe she was. She still wept; he felt he must draw nearer or go quite away. 'Eli.' He listened. 'Eli.'

'Yes.'

She checked her weeping. But he did not know what to say more, and was silent.

'What do you want?' she whispered, half turning towards him.

'It's something—'

His voice trembled, and he stopped.

'What is it?'

'You mustn't refuse... I would ask you...'

'Is it the song?'

'No... Eli, I wish so much...' He heard her breathing fast and deeply... 'I wish so much... to hold one of your hands.'

She did not answer; he listened intently — drew nearer, and clasped a warm little hand which lay on the coverlet.

Then steps were heard coming up-stairs; they came nearer and nearer; the door was opened; and Arne unclasped his hand. It was the mother, who came in with a light. 'I think you're sitting too long in the dark,' she said, putting the candlestick on the table. But neither Eli nor Arne could bear the light; she turned her face to the pillow, and he shaded his eyes with his hand. 'Well, it pains a little at first, but it soon passes off,' said the mother.

Arne looked on the floor for something which he had not dropped, and then went down-stairs.

The next day, he heard that Eli intended to come down in the afternoon. He put his tools together, and said good-bye. When she came down he had gone.

XIII.

MARGIT CONSULTS THE
CLERGYMAN

Up between the mountains, the spring comes late. The post, who in winter passes along the high-road thrice a week, in April passes only once; and the highlanders know then that outside, the snow is shovelled away, the ice broken, the steamers are running, and the plough is struck into the earth. Here, the snow still lies six feet deep; the cattle low in their stalls; the birds arrive, but feel cold and hide themselves. Occasionally some traveller arrives, saying he has left his carriage down in the valley; he brings flowers, which he examines; he picked them by the wayside. The people watch the advance of the season, talk over their matters, and look up at the sun and round about, to see how much he is able to do each day. They scatter ashes on the snow, and think of those who are now picking flowers.

It was at this time of year, old Margit Kampen went one day to the parsonage, and asked whether she might speak to 'father.' She was invited into the study, where the clergyman — a slender, fair-haired, gentle-looking man, with large eyes and spectacles — received her kindly, recognized her, and asked her to sit down.

'Is there something the matter with Arne again?' he inquired, as if Arne had often been a subject of conversation between them.

'Oh, dear, yes! I haven't anything wrong to say about him; but yet it's so sad,' said Margit, looking deeply grieved.

'Has that longing come back again!'

'Worse than ever. I can hardly think he'll even stay with me till spring comes up here.'

'But he has promised never to go away from you.'

'That's true; but, dear me! he must now be his own master; and if his mind's set upon going away, go, he must. But whatever will become of me then?'

'Well, after all, I don't think he will leave you.'

'Well, perhaps not; but still, if he isn't happy at home? am I then to have it upon my conscience that I stand in his way? Sometimes I feel as if I ought even to ask him to leave.'

'How do you know he is longing now, more than ever?'

'Oh — by many things. Since the middle of the winter, he hasn't worked out in the parish a single day; but he has been to the town three times, and has stayed a long while each time. He scarcely ever talks now while he is at work, but he often used to do. He'll sit for hours alone at the little upstairs window, looking towards the ravine, and away over the mountains; he'll sit there all Sunday afternoon, and often when it's moonlight he sits there till late in the night.'

'Does he never read to you?'

'Yes, of course, he reads and sings to me every Sunday; but he seems rather in a hurry, save now and then when he gives almost too much of the thing.'

'Does he never talk over matters with you then?'

'Well, yes; but it's so seldom that I sit and weep alone between whiles. Then I dare say he notices it, for he begins talking, but it's only about trifles; never about anything serious.'

The Clergyman walked up and down the room; then he stopped and asked, 'But why, then, don't you talk to him about his matters?'

For a long while she gave no answer; she sighed several times, looked downwards and sideways, doubled up her handkerchief, and at last said, 'I've come here to speak to you, father, about something that's a great burden on my mind.'

'Speak freely; it will relieve you.'

'Yes, I know it will; for I've borne it alone now these many years, and it grows heavier each year.'

'Well, what is it, my good Margit?'

There was a pause, and then she said, 'I've greatly sinned against my son.'

She began weeping. The Clergyman came close to her; 'Confess it,' he said; 'and we will pray together that it may be forgiven.'

Margit sobbed and wiped her eyes, but began weeping again when she tried to speak. The Clergyman tried to comfort her, saying she could not have done anything very sinful, she doubtless was too hard upon herself, and so on. But Margit continued weeping, and could not begin her confession till the Clergyman seated himself by her side, and spoke still more encouragingly to her. Then after a while she began, 'The boy was ill-used when a child; and so he got this mind for travelling. Then he met with Christian — he who has grown so rich over there where they dig gold. Christian gave him so many books that he got quite a scholar; they used to sit together in the long evenings; and when Christian went away Arne wanted to go after him. But just at that time, the father died, and the lad promised never to leave me. But I was like a hen that's got a duck's egg to brood; when my duckling had burst his shell, he would go out on the wide water, and I was left on the bank, calling after him. If he didn't go away himself, yet his heart went away in his songs, and every morning I expected to find his bed empty.

'Then a letter from foreign parts came for him, and I felt sure it must be from Christian. God forgive me, but I kept it back! I thought there would be no more, but another came; and, as I had kept the first, I thought I must keep the second, too. But, dear me! it seemed as if they would burn a hole through the box where I had put them; and my thoughts were there from as soon as I opened my eyes in the morning till late at night when I shut them. And then — did you ever hear of anything worse! — a third letter came. I held it in my hand a quarter of an hour; I kept it in my bosom three days, weighing in my mind whether I should give it to him or put it with the others; but then I thought perhaps it would lure him away from me, and so I couldn't help putting it with the others. But now I felt miserable every day, not only about the letters in the box, but also for fear another might come. I was afraid of everybody who came to the house; when we were sitting together inside, I trembled whenever I heard the door go, for fear it might be somebody with a letter, and then he might get it. When he was away in the parish, I went about at home thinking he might perhaps get a letter while there, and then it would tell him about those that had already come. When I saw him coming home, I used to look at his face while he was yet a long way off, and, oh, dear! how happy I felt when he smiled; for then I knew he had got no letter. He had grown so handsome, like his father, only fairer, and more gentle-looking. And, then, he had such a voice; when he sat at the door in the evening-sun, singing towards the mountain ridge, and listening to the echo, I felt that life without him... I never could. If I only saw him, or knew he was somewhere near, and he seemed pretty happy, and would only give me a word now and then, I wanted nothing more on earth, and I wouldn't have shed one tear less.

'But just when he seemed to be getting on better with people, and felt happier among them, there came a message from the post-office that a fourth letter had come; and in it were two hundred dollars! I thought I should have fell flat down where I stood: what could I do? The letter, I might get rid of, 'twas true; but the money? For two or three nights I couldn't sleep for it; a little while I left it up-stairs, then, in the cellar behind a barrel, and once I was so overdone that I laid it in the window so that he might find it. But when I heard him coming, I took it back again. At last, however, I found a way: I gave him the money and told him it had been put out at interest in my mother's lifetime. He laid it out upon the land, just as I thought he would; and so it wasn't wasted. But that same harvest-time, when he was sitting at home one evening, he began talking about Christian, and wondering why he had so clean forgotten him.

'Now again the wound opened, and the money burned me so that I was obliged to go out of the room. I had sinned, and yet my sin had answered no end. Since then, I have hardly dared to look into his eyes, blessed as they are.

'The mother who has sinned against her own child is the most miserable of all mothers... and yet I did it only out of love... And so, I dare say, I shall be punished accordingly by the loss of what I love most. For since the middle of the winter, he has again taken to singing the tune that he used to sing when he was longing to go away; he has sung it ever since he was a lad, and whenever I hear it I grow pale. Then I feel I could give up all for him; and only see this.' She took from her bosom a piece of paper, unfolded it and gave it to the Clergyman. 'He now and then writes something here; I think it's some words to that tune... I brought it with me; for I can't myself read such small writing... will you look and see if there isn't something written about his going away...'

There was only one whole verse on the paper. For the second verse, there were only a few half-finished lines, as if the song was one he had forgotten, and was now coming into his memory again, line by line. The first verse ran thus:

'What shall I see if I ever go
Over the mountains high?
Now I can see but the peaks of snow,
Crowning the cliffs where the pine trees grow,
Waiting and longing to rise
Nearer the beckoning skies.'

'Is there anything about his going away?' asked Margit.

'Yes, it is about that,' replied the Clergyman, putting the paper down.

'Wasn't I sure of it! Ah me! I knew the tune!' She sat with folded hands, looking intently and anxiously into the Clergyman's face, while tear after tear fell down her cheeks.

The Clergyman knew no more what to do in the matter than she did. 'Well, I think the lad must be left alone in this case,' he said. 'Life can't be made different for his sake; but what he will find in it must depend upon himself; now, it seems, he wishes to go away in search of life's good.'

'But isn't that just what the old crone did?'

'The old crone?'

'Yes; she who went away to fetch the sunshine, instead of making windows in the wall to let it in.'

The Clergyman was much astonished at Margit's words, and so he had been before, when she came speak to him on this subject; but, indeed, she had thought of hardly anything else for eight years.

'Do you think he'll go away? what am I to do? and the money? and the letters?' All these questions crowded upon her at once.

'Well, as to the letters, that wasn't quite right. Keeping back what belonged to your son, can't be justified. But it was still worse to make a fellow Christian appear in a bad light when he didn't deserve it; and especially as he was one whom Arne was so fond of, and who loved him so dearly in return. But we will pray God to forgive you; we will both pray.'

Margit still sat with her hands folded, and her head bent down.

'How I should pray him to forgive me, if I only knew he would stay!' she said: surely, she was confounding our Lord with Arne. The Clergyman, however, appeared as if he did not notice it.

'Do you intend to confess it to him directly?' he asked.

She looked down, and said in a low voice, 'I should much like to wait a little if I dared.'

The Clergyman turned aside with a smile, and asked, 'Don't you believe your sin becomes greater, the longer you delay confessing it?'

She pulled her handkerchief about with both hands, folded it into a very small square, and tried to fold it into a still smaller one, but could not.

'If I confess about the letters, I'm afraid he'll go away.'

'Then, you dare not rely upon our Lord?'

'Oh, yes, I do, indeed,' she said hurriedly; and then she added in a low voice, 'but still, if he were to go away from me?'

'Then, I see you are more afraid of his going away than of continuing to sin?'

Margit had unfolded her handkerchief again; and now she put it to her eyes, for she began weeping. The Clergyman remained for a while looking at her silently; then he went on, 'Why, then, did you tell me all this, if it was not to lead to anything?' He waited long, but she did not answer. 'Perhaps you thought your sin would become less when you had confessed it?'

'Yes, I did,' she said, almost in a whisper, while her head bent still lower upon her breast.

The Clergyman smiled and rose. 'Well, well, my good Margit, take courage; I hope all will yet turn out for the best.'

'Do you think so?' she asked, looking up; and a sad smile passed over her tear-marked face.

'Yes, I do; I believe God will no longer try you. You will have joy in your old age, I am sure.'

'If I might only keep the joy I have!' she said; and the Clergyman thought she seemed unable to fancy any greater happiness than living in that constant anxiety. He smiled and filled his pipe.

'If we had but a little girl, now, who could take hold on him, then I'm sure he would stay.'

'You may be sure I've thought of that,' she said, shaking her head.

'Well, there's Eli Böen; she might be one who would please him.'

'You may be sure I've thought of that.' She rocked the upper part of her body backwards and forwards.

'If we could contrive that they might oftener see each other here at the parsonage?'

'You may be sure I've thought of that!' She clapped her hands and looked at the Clergyman with a smile all over her face. He stopped while he was lighting his pipe.

'Perhaps this, after all, was what brought you here to-day?'

She looked down, put two fingers into the folded handkerchief, and pulled out one corner of it.

'Ah, well, God help me, perhaps it was this I wanted.'

The Clergyman walked up and down, and smiled. 'Perhaps, too, you came for the same thing the last time you were here?'

She pulled out the corner of the handkerchief still farther, and hesitated awhile. 'Well, as you ask me, perhaps I did — yes.'

The Clergyman went on smoking. 'Then, too, it was to carry this point that you confessed at last the thing you had on your conscience.'

She spread out the handkerchief to fold it up smoothly again. 'No; ah, no; that weighed so heavily upon me, I felt I must tell it to you, father.'

'Well, well, my dear Margit, we will talk no more about it.'

Then, while he was walking up and down, he suddenly added, 'Do you think you would of yourself have come out to me with this wish of yours?'

'Well — I had already come out with so much, that I dare say this, too, would have come out at last.'

The Clergyman laughed, but he did not tell her what he thought. After a while he stood still. 'Well, we will manage this matter for you, Margit,' he said.

'God bless you for it!' She rose to go, for she understood he had now said all he wished to say.

'And we will look after them a little.'

'I don't know how to thank you enough,' she said, taking his hand and courtesying.

'God be with you!' he replied.

She wiped her eyes with the handkerchief, went towards the door, courtesied again, and said, 'Good bye,' while she slowly opened and shut it. But so lightly as she went towards Kampen that day, she had not gone for many, many years. When she had come far enough to see the thick smoke curling up cheerfully from the chimney, she blessed the house, the whole place, the Clergyman and Arne — and remembered they were going to have her favourite dish, smoked ham, for dinner.

XIV.

FINDING A LOST SONG

Kampen was a beautiful place. It was situated in the middle of a plain, bordered on the one side by a ravine, and on the other, by the high-road; just beyond the road was a thick wood, with a mountain ridge rising behind it, while high above all stood blue mountains crowned with snow. On the other side of the ravine also was a wide range of mountains, running round the Swart-water on the side where Böen was situated: it grew higher as it ran towards Kampen, but then turned suddenly sidewards, forming the broad valley called the Lower-tract, which began here, for Kampen was the last place in the Upper-tract.

The front door of the dwelling-house opened towards the road, which was about two thousand paces off, and a path with leafy birch-trees on both sides led thither. In front of the house was a little garden, which Arne managed according to the rules given in his books. The cattle-houses and barns were nearly all new-built, and stood to the left hand, forming a square. The house was two stories high, and was painted red, with white window-frames and doors; the roof was of turf with many small plants growing upon it, and on the ridge was a vane-spindle, where turned an iron cock with a high raised tail.

Spring had come to the mountain-tracts. It was Sunday morning; the weather was mild and calm, but the air was somewhat heavy, and the mist lay low on the forest, though Margit said it would rise later in the day. Arne had read the sermon, and sung the hymns to his mother, and he felt better for them himself. Now he stood ready dressed to go to the parsonage. When he opened the door the fresh smell of the leaves met him; the garden lay dewy and bright in the morning breeze, but from the ravine sounded the roaring of the waterfall, now in lower, then again in louder booms, till all around seemed to tremble.

Arne walked upwards. As he went farther from the fall, its booming became less awful, and soon it lay over the landscape like the deep tones of an organ.

'God be with him wherever he goes!' the mother said, opening the window and looking after him till he disappeared behind the shrubs. The mist had gradually risen, the sun shone bright, the fields and garden became full of fresh life, and the things Arne had sown and tended grew and sent up odor and gladness to his mother. 'Spring is beautiful to those who have had a long winter,' she said, looking away over the fields, as if in thought.

Arne had no positive errand at the parsonage, but he thought he might go there to ask about the newspapers which he shared with the Clergyman. Recently he had read the names of several Norwegians who had been successful in gold digging in America, and among them was Christian. His relations had long since left the place, but Arne had lately heard a rumor that they expected him to come home soon. About this, also, Arne thought he might hear at the parsonage; and if Christian had already returned, he would go down and see him between spring and hay-harvest. These thoughts occupied his mind till he came far enough to see the Swart-water and Böen on the other side. There, too, the mist had risen, but it lay lingering on the mountain-sides, while their peaks rose clear above, and the sunbeams played on the plain; on the right hand, the shadow of the wood darkened the water, but before the houses the lake had strewed its white sand on the flat shore. All at once, Arne fancied himself in the red-painted house with the white doors and windows, which he had taken as a model for his own. He did not think of those first gloomy days he had passed there, but only of that summer they both saw — he and Eli — up beside her sick-bed. He had not been there since; nor would he have gone for the whole world. If his thoughts but touched on that time, he turned crimson; yet he thought of it many times a day; and if anything could have driven him away from the parish, it was this.

He strode onwards, as if to flee from his thoughts; but the farther he went, the nearer he came to Böen, and the more he looked at it. The mist had disappeared, the sky shone bright between the frame of mountains, the birds floated in the sunny air, calling to each other, and the fields laughed with millions of flowers; here no thundering waterfall bowed the gladness to submissive awe, but full of life it gambolled and sang without check or pause.

Arne walked till he became glowing hot; then he threw himself down on the grass beneath the shadow of a hill and looked towards Böen, but he soon turned away again to avoid seeing it. Then he heard a song above him, so wonderfully clear as he had never heard a song before. It came floating over the meadows, mingled with the chattering of the birds, and he had scarcely recognized the tune ere he recognized the words also: the tune was the one he loved better than any; the words were those he had borne in his mind ever since he was a boy, and had forgotten that same day they were brought forth. He sprang up as if he would catch them, but then stopped and listened while verse after verse came streaming down to him:

'What shall I see if I ever go
Over the mountains high?
Now, I can see but the peaks of snow,
Crowning the cliffs where the pine-trees grow,
Waiting and longing to rise
Nearer the beckoning skies.

'Th' eagle is rising afar away,
Over the mountains high,
Rowing along in the radiant day
With mighty strokes to his distant prey,
Where he will, swooping downwards,
Where he will, sailing onwards.

'Apple-tree, longest thou not to go
Over the mountains high?
Gladly thou growest in summer's glow,
Patiently waitest through winter's snow:
Though birds on thy branches swing,
Thou knowest not what they sing.

'He who has twenty years longed to flee
Over the mountains high —
He who beyond them, never will see,

Smaller, and smaller, each year must be:
He hears what the birds, say
While on thy boughs they play.

'Birds, with your chattering, why did ye come
Over the mountains high?
Beyond, in a sunnier land ye could roam,
And nearer to heaven could build your home;
Why have ye come to bring
Longing, without your wing?

'Shall I, then, never, never flee
Over the mountains high?
Rocky walls, will ye always be
Prisons until ye are tombs for me? —
Until I lie at your feet
Wrapped in my winding-sheet?

'Away! I will away, afar away,
Over the mountains high!
Here, I am sinking lower each day,
Though my Spirit has chosen the loftiest way;
Let her in freedom fly;
Not, beat on the walls and die!

'Once, I know, I shall journey far
Over the mountains high.
Lord, is thy door already ajar?
Dear is the home where thy saved ones are;
But bar it awhile from me,
And help me to long for Thee.'

Arne stood listening till the sound of the last verse, the last words died away; then he heard the birds sing and play again, but he dared not move. Yet he must find out who had been singing, and he lifted his foot and walked on, so carefully that he did not hear the grass rustle. A little butterfly settled on a flower at his feet, flew up and settled a little way before him, flew up and settled again, and so on all over the hill. But soon he came to a thick bush and stopped; for a bird flew out of it with a frightened 'quitt, quitt!' and rushed away over the sloping hill-side. Then she who was sitting there looked up; Arne stooped low down, his heart throbbed till he heard its beats, he held his breath, and was afraid to stir a leaf; for it was Eli whom he saw.

After a long while he ventured to look up again; he wished to draw nearer, but he thought the bird perhaps had its nest under the bush, and he was afraid he might tread on it. Then he peeped between the leaves as they blew aside and closed again. The sun shone full upon her. She wore a close-fitting black dress with long white sleeves, and a straw hat like those worn by boys. In her lap a book was lying with a heap of wild flowers upon it; her right hand was listlessly playing with them as if she were in thought, and her left supported her head. She was looking away towards the place where the bird had flown, and she seemed as if she had been weeping.

Anything more beautiful, Arne had never seen or dreamed of in all his life; the sun, too, had spread its gold over her and the place; and the song still hovered round her, so that Arne thought, breathed — nay, even his heart beat, in time with it. It seemed so strange that the song which bore all his longing, he had forgotten, but she had found.

A tawny wasp flew round her in circles many times, till at last she saw it and frightened it away with a flower-stalk, which she put up as often as it came before her. Then she took up the book and opened it, but she soon closed it again, sat as before, and began to hum another song. He could hear it was 'The Tree's early leaf-buds,' though she often made mistakes, as if she did not quite remember either the words or the tune. The verse she knew best was the last one, and so she often repeated it; but she sang it thus:

'The Tree bore his berries, so mellow and red:
"May I gather thy berries?" a sweet maiden said.
"Yes; all thou canst see;
Take them; all are for thee,"
Said the Tree — trala — lala, trala, lala — said.'

Then she suddenly sprang up, scattering all the flowers around her, and sang till the tune trembled through the air, and might have been heard at Böen. Arne had thought of coming forwards when she began singing; he was just about to do so when she jumped up; then he felt he must come, but she went away. Should he call? No — yes! No! — There she skipped over the hillocks singing; here her hat fell off, there she took it up again; here she picked a flower, there she stood deep in the highest grass.

'Shall I call? She's looking up here!'

He stooped down. It was a long while ere he ventured to peep out again; at first he only raised his head; he could not see her: he rose to his knees; still he could not see her: he stood upright; no she was gone. He thought himself a miserable fellow; and some of the tales he had heard at the nutting-party came into his mind.

Now he would not go to the parsonage. He would not have the newspapers; would not know anything about Christian. He would not go home; he would go nowhere; he would do nothing.

'Oh, God, I am so unhappy!' he said.

He sprang up again and sang 'The Tree's early leaf-buds' till the mountains resounded.

Then he sat down where she had been sitting, and took up the flowers she had picked, but he flung them away again down the hill on every side. Then he wept. It was long since he had done so; this struck him, and made him weep still more. He would go far away, that he would; no, he would not go away! He thought he was very unhappy; but when he asked himself why, he could hardly tell. He looked round. It was a lovely day; and the Sabbath rest lay over all. The lake was without a ripple; from the houses the curling smoke had begun to rise; the partridges one after another had ceased calling, and though the little birds continued their twittering, they went towards the shade of the wood; the dewdrops were gone, and the grass looked grave; not a breath of wind stirred the drooping leaves; and the sun was near the meridian. Almost before he knew, he found himself seated putting together a little song; a sweet tune offered itself for it; and while his heart was strangely full of gentle feelings, the tune went and came till words linked themselves to it and begged to be sung, if only for once.

He sang them gently, sitting where Eli had sat:

'He went in the forest the whole day long,
    The whole day long;

For there he had heard such a wondrous song,
    A wondrous song.

'He fashioned a flute from a willow spray,
    A willow spray,
To see if within it the sweet tune lay,
    The sweet tune lay.

'It whispered and told him its name at last,
    Its name at last;
But then, while he listened, away it passed,
    Away it passed.

'But oft when he slumbered, again it stole,
    Again it stole,
With touches of love upon his soul,
    Upon his soul.

'Then he tried to catch it, and keep it fast,
    And keep it fast;
But he woke, and away I' the night it passed,
    I' the night it passed.

'"My Lord, let me pass in the night, I pray,
    In the night, I pray;
For the tune has taken my heart away,
    My heart away.'

'Then answered the Lord, "It is thy friend,
    It is thy friend,
Though not for an hour shall thy longing end,
    Thy longing end;

"'And all the others are nothing to thee,
     Nothing to thee,
To this that thou seekest and never shalt see,
     Never shalt see.'"

XV.

SOMEBODY'S FUTURE HOME

'Good bye,' said Margit at the Clergyman's door. It was a Sunday evening in advancing summer-time; the Clergyman had returned from church, and Margit had been sitting with him till now, when it was seven o'clock. 'Good bye, Margit,' said the Clergyman. She hurried down the door-steps and into the yard; for she had seen Eli Böen playing there with her brother and the Clergyman's son.

'Good evening,' said Margit, stopping; 'and God bless you all.'

'Good evening,' answered Eli. She blushed crimson and wanted to leave off the game; the boys begged her to keep on, but she persuaded them to let her go for that evening.

'I almost think I know you,' said Margit.

'Very likely.'

'Isn't it Eli Böen?'

Yes, it was.

'Dear me! you're Eli Böen; yes, now I see you're like your mother.'

Eli's auburn hair had come unfastened, and hung down over her neck and shoulders; she was hot and as red as a cherry, her bosom fluttered up and down, and she could scarcely speak, but laughed because she was so out of breath.

'Well, young folks should be merry,' said Margit, feeling happy as she looked at her. 'P'r'aps you don't know me?'

If Margit had not been her senior, Eli would probably have asked her name, but now she only said she did not remember having seen her before.

'No; I dare say not: old folks don't go out much. But my son, p'r'aps you know a little — Arne Kampen; I'm his mother,' said Margit, with a stolen glance at Eli, who suddenly looked grave and breathed slowly. 'I'm pretty sure he worked at Böen once.'

Yes, Eli thought he did.

'It's a fine evening; we turned our hay this morning, and got it in before I came away; it's good weather indeed for everything.'

'There will be a good hay-harvest this year,' Eli suggested.

'Yes, you may well say that; everything's getting on well at Böen, I suppose?'

'We have got in all our hay.'

'Oh, yes, I dare say you have; your folks work well, and they have plenty of help. Are you going home to-night?'

No, she was not.

'Couldn't you go a little way with me? I so seldom have anybody to talk to; and it will be all the same to you, I suppose?'

Eli excused herself, saying she had not her jacket on.

'Well, it's a shame to ask such a thing the first time of seeing anybody; but one must put up with old folks'' ways.'

Eli said she would go; she would only fetch her jacket first.

It was a close-fitting jacket, which when fastened looked like a dress with a bodice; but now she fastened only two of the lower hooks, because she was so hot. Her fine linen bodice had a little turned-down collar, and was fastened with a silver stud in the shape of a bird with spread wings. Just such a one, Nils, the tailor, wore the first time Margit danced with him.

'A pretty stud,' she said, looking at it.

'Mother gave it me.'

'Ah, I thought so,' Margit said, helping her with the jacket.

They walked onwards over the fields. The hay was lying in heaps; and Margit took up a handful, smelled it, and thought it was very good. She asked about the cattle at the parsonage, and this led her to ask also about the live stock at Böen, and then she told how much they had at Kampen. 'The farm has improved very much these last few years, and it can still be made twice as large. He keeps twelve milch-cows now, and he could keep several more, but he reads so many books and manages according to them, and so he will have the cows fed in such a first-rate way.'

Eli, as might be expected, said nothing to all this; and Margit then asked her age. She was above twenty.

'Have you helped in the house-work? Not much, I dare say — you look so spruce.'

Yes, she had helped a good deal, especially of late.

'Well, it's best to use one's self to do a little of everything; when one gets a large house of one's own, there's a great deal to be done. But, of course, when one finds good help already in the house before her, why, it doesn't matter so much.'

Now Eli thought she must go back; for they had gone a long way beyond the grounds of the parsonage.

'It still wants some hours to sunset; it would be kind it you would chat a little longer with me.' And Eli went on.

Then Margit began to talk about Arne. 'I don't know if you know much of him. He could teach you something about everything, he could; dear me, what a deal he has read!'

Eli owned she knew he had read a great deal.

'Yes; and that's only the least thing that can be said of him; but the way he has behaved to his mother all his days, that's something more, that is. If the old saying is true, that he who's good to his mother is good to his wife, the one Arne chooses won't have much to complain of.'

Eli asked why they had painted the house before them with grey paint.

'Ah, I suppose they had no other; I only wish Arne may sometime be rewarded for all his kindness to his mother. When he has a wife, she ought to be kind-hearted as well as a good scholar. What are you looking for, child?'

'I only dropped a little twig I had.'

'Dear me! I think of many things, you may be sure, while I sit alone in yonder wood. If ever he takes home a wife who brings blessings to house and man, then I know many a poor soul will be glad that day.'

They were both silent, and walked on without looking at each other; but soon Eli stopped.

'What's the matter?'

'One of my shoe-strings has come down.'

Margit waited a long while till at last the string was tied.

'He has such queer ways,' she began again; 'he got cowed while he was a child, and so he has got into the way of

142

thinking over everything by himself, and those sort of folks haven't courage to come forward.'

Now Eli must indeed go back, but Margit said that Kampen was only half a mile off; indeed, not so far, and that Eli must see it, as too she was so near. But Eli thought it would be late that day.

'There'll be sure to be somebody to bring you home.'

'No, no,' Eli answered quickly, and would go back.

'Arne's not at home, it's true,' said Margit; 'but there's sure to be somebody else about;' and Eli had now less objection to it.

'If only I shall not be too late,' she said.

'Yes, if we stand here much longer talking about it, it may be too late, I dare say.' And they went on. 'Being brought up at the Clergyman's, you've read a great deal, I dare say?'

Yes, she had.

'It'll be of good use when you have a husband who knows less.'

No; that, Eli thought she would never have.

'Well, no; p'r'aps, after all, it isn't the best thing; but still folks about here haven't much learning.'

Eli asked if it was Kampen, she could see straight before her.

'No; that's Gransetren, the next place to the wood; when we come farther up you'll see Kampen. It's a pleasant place to live at, is Kampen, you may be sure; it seems a little out of the way, it's true; but that doesn't matter much, after all.'

Eli asked what made the smoke that rose from the wood.

'It comes from a houseman's cottage, belonging to Kampen: a man named Opplands-Knut lives there. He went about lonely till Arne gave him that piece of land to clear. Poor Arne! he knows what it is to be lonely.'

Soon they came far enough to see Kampen.

'Is that Kampen?' asked Eli, standing still and pointing.

'Yes, it is,' said the mother; and she, too, stood still. The sun shone full in their faces, and they shaded their eyes as they looked down over the plain. In the middle of it stood the red-painted house with its white window-frames; rich green cornfields lay between the pale new-mown meadows, where some of the hay was already set in stacks; near the cow-house, all was life and stir; the cows, sheep and goats were coming home; their bells tinkled, the dogs barked, and the milkmaids called; while high above all, rose the grand tune of the waterfall from the ravine. The farther Eli went, the more this filled her ears, till at last it seemed quite awful to her; it whizzed and roared through her head, her heart throbbed violently, and she became bewildered and dizzy, and then felt so subdued that she unconsciously began to walk with such small timid steps that Margit begged her to come on a little faster. She started. 'I never heard anything like that fall,' she said; 'I'm quite frightened.'

'You'll soon get used to it; and at last you'll even miss it.'

'Do you think so?'

'Well, you'll see.' And Margit smiled.

'Come, now, we'll first look at the cattle,' she said, turning downwards from the road, into the path. 'Those trees on each side, Nils planted; he wanted to have everything nice, did Nils; and so does Arne; look, there's the garden he has laid out.'

'Oh, how pretty!' exclaimed Eli, going quickly towards the garden fence.

'We'll look at that by-and-by,' said Margit; 'now we must go over to look at the creatures before they're locked in—' But Eli did not hear, for all her mind was turned to the garden. She stood looking at it till Margit called her once more; as she came along, she gave a furtive glance through the windows; but she could see no one inside.

They both went upon the barn steps and looked down at the cows, as they passed lowing into the cattle-house. Margit named them one by one to Eli, and told her how much milk each gave, and which would calve in the summer, and which would not. The sheep were counted and penned in; they were of a large foreign breed, raised from two lambs which Arne had got from the South. 'He aims at all such things,' said Margit, 'though one wouldn't think it of him.' Then they went into the barn, and looked at some hay which had been brought in, and Eli had to smell it; 'for such hay isn't to be found everywhere,' Margit said. She pointed from the barn-hatch to the fields, and told what kind of seed was sown on them, and how much of each kind. 'No less than three fields are new-cleared, and now, this first year, they're set with potatoes, just for the sake of the ground; over there, too, the land's new-cleared, but I suppose that soil's different, for there he has sown barley; but then he has strewed burnt turf over it for manure, for he attends to all such things. Well, she that comes here will find things in good order, I'm sure.' Now they went out towards the dwelling-house; and Eli, who had answered nothing to all that Margit had told her about other things, when they passed the garden asked if she might go into it; and when she got leave to go, she begged to pick a flower or two. Away in one corner was a little garden-seat;

she went over and sat down upon it — perhaps only to try it, for she rose directly.

'Now we must make haste, else we shall be too late,' said Margit, as she stood at the house-door. Then they went in. Margit asked if Eli would not take some refreshment, as this was the first time she had been at Kampen; but Eli turned red and quickly refused. Then they looked round the room, which was the one Arne and the mother generally used in the day-time; it was not very large, but cosy and pleasant, with windows looking out on the road. There were a clock and a stove; and on the wall hung Nils" fiddle, old and dark, but with new strings; beside it hung some guns belonging to Arne, English fishing-tackle and other rare things, which the mother took down and showed to Eli, who looked at them and touched them. The room was without painting, for this Arne did not like; neither was there any in the large pretty room which looked towards the ravine, with the green mountains on the other side, and the blue peaks in the background. But the two smaller rooms in the wing were both painted; for in them the mother would live when she became old, and Arne brought a wife into the house: Margit was very fond of painting, and so in these rooms the ceilings were painted with roses, and her name was painted on the cupboards, the bedsteads, and on all reasonable and unreasonable places; for it was Arne himself who had done it. They went into the kitchen, the store-room, and the bake-house; and now they had only to go into the up-stairs rooms; 'all the best things were there,' the mother said.

These were comfortable rooms, corresponding with those below, but they were new and not yet taken into use, save one which looked towards the ravine. In them hung and stood all sorts of household things not in every-day use. Here hung a lot of fur coverlets and other bedclothes; and the mother took hold of them and lifted them; so did Eli, who looked at all of them with pleasure, examined some of them twice, and asked questions about them, growing all the while more interested.

'Now we'll find the key of Arne's room,' said the mother, taking it from under a chest where it was hidden. They went into the room; it looked towards the ravine; and once more the awful booming of the waterfall met their ears, for the window was open. They could see the spray rising between the cliffs, but not the fall itself, save in one place farther up, where a huge fragment of rock had fallen into it just where the torrent came in full force to take its last leap into the depths below. The upper side of this fragment was covered with fresh sod; and a few pine-cones had dug themselves into it, and had grown up to trees, rooted into the crevices. The wind had shaken and twisted them; and the fall had dashed against them, so that they had not a sprig lower than eight feet from their roots: they were gnarled and bent; yet they stood, rising high between the rocky walls. When Eli looked out from the window, these trees first caught her eye; next, she saw the snowy peaks rising far beyond behind the green mountains. Then her eyes passed over the quiet fertile fields back to the room; and the first thing she saw there was a large bookshelf. There were so many books on it that she scarcely believed the Clergyman had more. Beneath it was a cupboard, where Arne kept his money. The mother said money had been left to them twice already, and if everything went right they would have some more. 'But, after all, money's not the best thing in the world; he may get what's better still,' she added.

There were many little things in the cupboard which were amusing to see, and Eli looked at them all, happy as a child. Then the mother showed her a large chest where Arne's clothes lay, and they, too, were taken out and looked at. Margit patted Eli on the shoulder. 'I've never seen you till to-day, and yet I'm already so fond of you, my child,' she said, looking affectionately into her eyes. Eli had scarcely time to feel a little bashful, before Margit pulled her by the hand and said in a low voice, 'Look at that little red chest; there's something very choice in that, you may be sure.'

Eli glanced towards the chest: it was a little square one, which she thought she would very much like to have.

'He doesn't want me to know what's in that chest,' the mother whispered; 'and he always hides the key.' She went to some clothes that hung on the wall, took down a velvet waistcoat, looked in the pocket, and there found the key.

'Now come and look,' she whispered; and they went gently, and knelt down before the chest. As soon as the mother opened it, so sweet an odor met them that Eli clapped her hands even before she had seen anything. On the top was spread a handkerchief, which the mother took away. 'Here, look,' she whispered, taking out a fine black silk neckerchief such as men do not wear. 'It looks just as if it was meant for a girl,' the mother said. Eli spread it upon her lap and looked at it, but did not say a word. 'Here's one more,' the mother said. Eli could not help taking it up; and then the mother insisted upon trying it on her, though Eli drew back and held her head down. She did not know what she would not have given for such a neckerchief; but she thought of something more than that. They folded them up again, but slowly.

'Now, look here,' the mother said, taking out some handsome ribands. 'Everything seems as if it was for a girl.' Eli blushed crimson, but she said nothing. 'There's some more things yet,' said the mother, taking out some fine black cloth for a dress; 'it's fine, I dare say,' she added, holding it up to the light. Eli's hands trembled, her chest heaved, she felt the blood rushing to her head, and she would fain have turned away, but that she could not well do.

'He has bought something every time he has been to town,' continued the mother. Eli could scarcely bear it any longer; she looked from one thing to another in the chest, and then again at the cloth, and her face burned. The next thing the mother took out was wrapped in paper; they unwrapped it, and found a small pair of shoes. Anything like them, they had never seen, and the mother wondered how they could be made. Eli said nothing; but when she touched the shoes her fingers left warm marks on them. 'I'm hot, I think,' she whispered. The mother put all the things carefully together.

'Doesn't it seem just as if he had bought them all, one after another, for somebody he was afraid to give them to?' she said, looking at Eli. 'He has kept them here in this chest — so long.' She laid them all in the chest again, just as they were before. 'Now we'll see what's here in the compartment,' she said, opening the lid carefully, as if she were now going to show Eli something specially beautiful.

When Eli looked she saw first a broad buckle for a waistband, next, two gold rings tied together, and a hymn-book bound in velvet and with silver clasps; but then she saw nothing more, for on the silver of the book she had seen graven in small letters, 'Eli Baardsdatter Böen.'

The mother wished her to look at something else; she got no answer, but saw tear after tear dropping down upon the silk neckerchief and spreading over it. She put down the *sylgje** which she had in her hand, shut the lid, turned round and drew Eli to her. Then the daughter wept upon her breast, and the mother wept over her, without either of them saying any more.

A little while after, Eli walked by herself in the garden, while the mother was in the kitchen preparing something nice for supper; for now Arne would soon be at home. Then she came out in the garden to Eli, who sat tracing names on the sand with a stick. When she saw Margit, she smoothed the sand down over them, looked up and smiled; but she had been weeping.

'There's nothing to cry about, my child,' said Margit, caressing her; 'supper's ready now; and here comes Arne,' she added, as a black figure appeared on the road between the shrubs.

Eli stole in, and the mother followed her. The supper-table was nicely spread with dried meat, cakes and cream porridge; Eli did not look at it, however, but went away to a corner near the clock and sat down on a chair close to the wall, trembling at every sound. The mother stood by the table. Firm steps were heard on the flagstones, and a short, light step in the passage, the door was gently opened, and Arne came in.

The first thing he saw was Eli in the corner; he left hold on the door and stood still. This made Eli feel yet more confused; she rose, but then felt sorry she had done so, and turned aside towards the wall.

'Are you here?' said Arne, blushing crimson.

She held her hand before her face, as one does when the sun shines into the eyes.

'How did you come here?' he asked, advancing a few steps.

She put her hand down again, and turned a little towards him, but then bent her head and burst into tears.

'Why do you weep, Eli?' he asked, coming to her. She did not answer, but wept still more.

'God bless you, Eli!' he said, laying his arm round her. She leant her head upon his breast, and he whispered something down to her; she did not answer, but clasped her hands round his neck.

They stood thus for a long while; and not a sound was heard, save that of the fall which still gave its eternal warning, though distant and subdued. Then some one over against the table was heard weeping; Arne looked up: it was the mother; but he had not noticed her till then. 'Now, I'm sure you won't go away from me, Arne,' she said, coming across the floor to him; and she wept much, but it did her good, she said.

Later, when they had supped and said good-bye to the mother, Eli and Arne walked together along the road to the parsonage. It was one of those light summer nights when all things seem to whisper and crowd together, as if in fear. Even he who has from childhood been accustomed to such nights, feels strangely influenced by them, and goes about as if expecting something to happen: light is there, but not life.

Often the sky is tinged with blood-red, and looks out between the pale clouds like an eye that has watched. One seems to hear a whispering all around, but it comes only from one's own brain, which is over-excited. Man shrinks, feels his own littleness, and thinks of his God.

Those two who were walking here also kept close to each other; they felt as if they had too much happiness, and they feared it might be taken from them.

'I can hardly believe it,' Arne said.

'I feel almost the same,' said Eli, looking dreamily before her.

'Yet it's true,' he said, laying stress on each word; 'now I am no longer going about only thinking; for once I have done something.'

He paused a few moments, and then laughed, but not gladly. 'No, it was not I,' he said; 'it was mother who did it.'

He seemed to have continued this thought, for after a while he said, 'Up to this day I have done nothing; not taken my part in anything. I have looked on... and listened.'

He went on a little farther, and then said warmly, 'God be thanked that I have got through in this way... now people will not have to see many things which would not have been as they ought...' Then after a while he added, 'But if some one had not helped me, perhaps I should have gone on alone for ever.' He was silent.

'What do you think father will say, dear?' asked Eli, who had been busy with her own thoughts.

'I am going over to Böen early to-morrow morning,' said Arne;.'that, at any rate, I must do myself,' he added, determining he would now be cheerful and brave, and never think of sad things again; no, never! 'And, Eli, it was you who found my song in the nut-wood?' She laughed. 'And the tune I had made it for, you got hold of, too.'

'I took the one which suited it,' she said, looking down. He smiled joyfully and bent his face down to hers.

'But the other song you did not know?'

'Which?' she asked looking up...

'Eli... you mustn't be angry with me... but one day this spring... yes, I couldn't help it, I heard you singing on the parsonage-hill.'

She blushed and looked down, but then she laughed. 'Then, after all, you have been served just right,' she said.

'What do you mean?'

'Well — it was; nay, it wasn't my fault; it was your mother... well... another time...'

'Nay; tell it me now.'

She would not — then he stopped and exclaimed, 'Surely, you haven't been up-stairs?' He was so grave that she felt frightened, and looked down.

'Mother has perhaps found the key to that little chest?' he added in a gentle tone.

She hesitated, looked up and smiled, but it seemed as if only to keep back her tears; then he laid his arm round her neck and drew her still closer to him. He trembled, lights seemed flickering before his eyes, his head burned, he bent over her and his lips sought hers, but could hardly find them; he staggered, withdrew his arm, and turned aside, afraid to look at her. The clouds had taken such strange shapes; there was one straight before him which looked like a goat with two great horns, and standing on its hind legs; and there was the nose of an old woman with her hair tangled; and there was the picture of a big man, which was set slantwise, and then was suddenly rent... But just over the mountain the sky was blue and clear; the cliff stood gloomy, while the lake lay quietly beneath it, afraid to move; pale and misty it lay, forsaken both by sun and moon, but the wood went down to it, full of love just as before. Some birds woke and twittered half in sleep; answers came over from one copse and then from another, but there was no danger at hand, and they slept once more... there was peace all around. Arne felt its blessedness lying over him as it lay over the evening.

'Thou great, thou Almighty God!' he said, so that he heard the words himself, and he folded his hands, but went a little before Eli that she might not see it.

XVI.

THE DOUBLE WEDDING

It was in the end of harvest-time, and the corn was being carried. It was a bright day; there had been rain in the night and earlier in morning, but now the air was clear and mild as in summer-time. It was Saturday; yet many boats were steering over the Swart-water towards the church; the men, in their white shirt-sleeves, sat rowing, while the women, with light-coloured kerchiefs on their heads, sat in the stern and the forepart. But still more boats were steering towards Böen, in readiness to go out thence in procession; for to-day Baard Böen kept the wedding of his daughter, Eli, and Arne Nilsson Kampen.

The doors were all open, people went in and out, children with pieces of cake in their hands stood in the yard, fidgety about their new clothes, and looking distantly at each other; an old woman sat lonely and weeping on the steps of the storehouse: it was Margit Kampen. She wore a large silver ring, with several small rings fastened to the upper plate; and now and then she looked at it: Nils gave it her on their wedding-day, and she had never worn it since.

The purveyor of the feast and the two young brides-men — the Clergyman's son and Eli's brother — went about in the rooms offering refreshments to the wedding-guests as they arrived. Up-stairs in Eli's room, were the Clergyman's lady, the bride and Mathilde, who had come from town only to put on her bridal-dress and ornaments, for this they had promised each other from childhood. Arne was dressed in a fine cloth suit, round jacket, black hat, and a collar that Eli had made; and he was in one of the down-stairs rooms, standing at the window where she wrote 'Arne.' It was open, and he leant upon the sill, looking away over the calm water towards the distant bight and the church.

Outside in the passage, two met as they came from doing their part in the day's duties. The one came from the stepping-stones on the shore, where he had been arranging the church-boats; he wore a round black jacket of fine cloth, and blue frieze trousers, off which the dye came, making his hands blue; his white collar looked well against his fair face and long light hair; his high forehead was calm, and a quiet smile lay round his lips. It was Baard. She whom he met had just come from the kitchen, dressed ready to go to church. She was tall and upright, and came through the door somewhat hurriedly, but with a firm step; when she met Baard she stopped, and her mouth drew to one side. It was Birgit, the wife. Each had something to say to the other, but neither could find words for it. Baard was even more embarrassed than she; he smiled more and more, and at last turned towards the staircase, saying as he began to step up, 'Perhaps you'll come too.' And she went up after him. Here, up-stairs, was no one but themselves; yet Baard locked the door after them, and he was a long while about it. When at last he turned round, Birgit stood looking out from the window, perhaps to avoid looking in the room. Baard took from his breast-pocket a little silver cup, and a little bottle of wine, and poured out some for her. But she would not take any, though he told her it was wine the Clergyman had sent them. Then he drank some himself, but offered it to her several times while he was drinking. He corked the bottle, put it again into his pocket with the cup, and sat down on a chest.

He breathed deeply several times, looked down and said, 'I'm so happy-to-day; and I thought I must speak freely with you; it's a long while since I did so.'

Birgit stood leaning with one hand upon the window-sill. Baard went on, 'I've been thinking about Nils, the tailor, to-day; he separated us two; I thought it wouldn't go beyond our wedding, but it has gone farther. To-day, a son of his, well-taught and handsome, is taken into our family, and we have given him our only daughter. What now, if we, Birgit, were to keep our wedding once again, and keep it so that we can never more be separated?'

His voice trembled, and he gave a little cough. Birgit laid her head down upon her arm, but said nothing. Baard waited long, but he got no answer, and he had himself nothing more to say. He looked up and grew very pale, for she did not even turn her head. Then he rose.

At the same moment came a gentle knock at the door, and a soft voice asked, 'Are you coming now, mother?' It was Eli. Birgit raised her head, and, looking towards the door, she saw Baard's pale face. 'Are you coming now, mother?' was asked once more.

'Yes, now I am coming,' said Birgit in a broken voice, while she gave her hand to Baard, and burst into a violent flood of tears.

The two hands pressed each other; they were both toilworn now, but they clasped as firmly as if they had sought each other for twenty years. They were still locked together, when Baard and Birgit went to the door; and afterwards when the bridal train went down to the stepping-stones on the shore, and Arne gave his hand to Eli, Baard looked at them, and, against all custom, took Birgit by the hand and followed them with a bright smile.

But Margit Kampen went behind them lonely.

Baard was quite overjoyed that day. While he was talking with the rowers, one of them, who sat looking at the mountains behind, said how strange it was that even such a steep cliff could be clad. 'Ah, whether it wishes to be, or not, it must,' said Baard, looking all along the train till his eyes rested on the bridal pair and his wife.

'Who could have foretold this twenty years ago?' said he.

NOTES

p. 19. The *halling* is a Norwegian national dance, of which a description is given on p. 21. (Translators.)

p. 54. In Norway, certain public announcements are made before the church door on Sundays after service. (Translators.)

p. 79. 'Over the whole of Norway, the tradition is current of a supernatural being that dwells in the forests and mountains, called *huldre* or *Hulla*. She appears like a beautiful woman, and is usually clad in a blue petticoat and a white snood; but unfortunately has a long tail, which she anxiously tries to conceal when she is among people. She is fond of cattle, particularly brindled, of which she possesses a beautiful and thriving stock. They are without horns. She was once at a merrymaking, where every one was desirous of dancing with the handsome, strange damsel; but in the midst of the mirth, a young man, who had just begun a dance with her, happened to cast his eye on her tail. Immediately guessing whom he had got for a partner, he was not a little terrified; but, collecting himself, and unwilling to betray her, he merely said to her when the dance was over, "Fair maid, you will lose your garter." She instantly vanished, but afterwards rewarded the silent and considerate youth with beautiful presents and a good breed of cattle. The idea entertained of this being is not everywhere the same, but varies considerably in different parts of Norway. In some places she is described as a handsome female when seen in front, but is hollow behind, or else blue; while in others she is known by the name of Skogmerte, and is said to be blue, but clad in a green petticoat, and probably corresponds to the Swedish Skogsnyfoor. Her song — a sound often heard among the mountains — is said to be hollow and mournful, differing therein from the music of the subterranean beings, which is described by earwitnesses as cheerful and fascinating. But she is not everywhere regarded as a solitary wood nymph. *huldremen* and *huldrefolk* are also spoken of, who live together in the mountains, and are almost identical with the subterranean people. In Hardanger the *huldre* people are always clad in green, but their cattle are blue, and may be taken when a grown-up person casts his belt over them. They give abundance of milk. The *huldre*s take possession of the forsaken pasture-spots in the mountains, and invite people into their mounds, where delightful music is to be heard.' (*Thorpe's Northern Mythology*.)

p. 100. As on p. 72.

p. 150. *sylgje*, a peculiar kind of brooch worn in Norway. (Translators.)

Cockatrice Books

Y diawl a'm llaw chwith

*Published as part of the Cymru'r Byd series, celebrating the
literature of Wales and the world.*

The cockatrice is hatched from a cockerel's egg, and
resembles a dragon the size and shape of a cockerel. The
English word is derived from the Latin *calcatrix*, but in Welsh
it is called *ceiliog neidr*: 'adder-cock.' Its touch, breath and
glance are lethal.

There is a saying in Welsh, *Y ddraig goch ddyry cychwyn,* which
means, 'The red dragon leads the way.' The cockatrice spits
at your beery patriotism.

www.cockatrice-books.com

HIS HAPPINESS
by Bjørnstjerne Bjørnson
Translated by Sivert and Elizabeth Hjerleid

The peasant son of a village peasant sets his heart on marrying the daughter of a local land-owner. A young lad aspires to scale the crags above his valley to the place where the eagles nest, and four short encounters between a father and the parish priest sketch the story of a young man's life.

With a timeless simplicity that recalls the work of Margiad Evans or Caradoc Evans, and with a love of the Norwegian land and people, these three stories represent the work of one of the forgotten masters of European literature.

Published as part of the Cymru'r Byd *series: celebrating the literature of Wales and the world.*

THE SCARLET FLOWER AND OTHER STORIES
by Vsevolod Garshin
Translated by E. L. Voynich and Rowland Smith

A young writer lies wounded, hungry and dying of thirst, by the body of the Turkish soldier he has killed. A volunteer and private on the long march to Bulgaria assaults the officer who thought of him as an equal and a friend. A prostitute scorns the marriage that could save her life, preferring death to shame, and a patient in a lunatic asylum begins a solitary battle against the flower which is the source of all evil and suffering in the world. Combining the social awareness of Orwell or Gorky with the artistry of Turgenev, these stories demonstrate the work of a writer uniquely attuned to the sufferings of his people and the imperatives of his art.

'Gogol, Turgenev, Tolstoi, Dostoevsky... None of our great masters created, at Garshin's age, anything better than his work, and none can stand as so true and painfully effective a representative of the spirit of our troubled time.'

S. Stepniak

MY PEOPLE
By Caradoc Evans

A respected member of the chapel, Zion, pronounces his wife mad and confines her to the hayloft. A man rides to the April fair to buy a heifer without blemish and acquire a wife. And God appears in a dream to a lonely farmhand, and tells him to dig for a talent under Old Shaci's ruined hut.

These short stories depict the poverty and hardship endured by the peasants of west Wales in the Nineteenth Century. But they also reveal the meanness and cruelty of lives lived in ignorance, caught between the desire for love and the fear of violence, and oppressed by the dark power of the chapel minister and the idol he represents. First published in 1915, to great outrage and great acclaim, they retain their timeless quality as classics and their power to shock.

THE WHITE FARM AND OTHER STORIES
By Geraint Goodwin

A farmer's orphan attends the auction of her stock with the man she intends to marry and the man she loves. A retired boxer who once killed a man is challenged to fight by the local drunk. Two men and a woman stand facing each other on the wasteground behind a country fair, and a successful businessman journeys home to be reconciled with the woman he once raped.

In his eye for the unremarked drama of Welsh lives, Geraint Goodwin is the equal of Caradoc Evans or Margiad Evans, yet his feel for atmosphere and detail is reminiscent of Turgenev. In the borderlands between England and Wales, men and women reach out to each other, groping for unity whilst riven by the gap between convention and passion.

REASONING: TWENTY STORIES
by Rob Mimpriss

Reasoning is the first of three collections by Rob Mimpriss. It is followed by *For His Warriors* and *Prayer at the End.*

An old man tries to assess his guilt in the marriage his daughter has destroyed. A young man tries to understand why, in the same family, he should be both hated and loved. A seventeenth-century Puritan preacher and a Cardiff woman facing divorce unite in their call to 'know your innermost heart,' while a Romanian dissident under Ceauşescu and a Welsh-language activist find themselves outwardly liberated but inwardly still in chains.

'Through the stealthy movements of his prose, Rob Mimpriss enacts the quiet enigma of people's lives and relationships. The result is an understated fiction of compelling intensity.'
M Wynn Thomas

FOR HIS WARRIORS: THIRTY STORIES
by Rob Mimpriss

For His Warriors is the second of three collections by Rob Mimpriss. It is preceded by *Reasoning* and followed by *Prayer at the End.*

A Welsh farmer's wife during the Second World War kills the landgirl her husband has taken as his lover. A leader of the Cornish-language revival commits her last act of protest the day Russian troops march into Berlin. A lonely man on the waterfront in Llandudno wonders whether he or his girlfriend will be first to die of Aids, and a bored man in a restaurant in Cardiff Bay invents a story of arrest and torture to amuse his petulant lover.

'Both humour and pity often arise from the characters' inability to understand themselves and those close to them. In suggesting both the truth and the self-deception Mimpriss not only engages our sympathy but makes us question our assumptions about ourselves.'

Caroline Clark, gwales.com

PRAYER AT THE END: TWENTY-THREE STORIES
by Rob Mimpriss

Prayer at the End is the third of three collections by Rob Mimpriss. It is preceded by *Reasoning* and *For His Warriors*.

A cigarette quenched in the Menai Strait makes a man vow to live a selfish life. The memory of an unborn twin makes a man regret the selfish life he has lived. An elderly shopkeeper befriends the teenagers outside his shop, and a lonely householder sets out to confront the trespassers on his land.

'In the most seemingly unremarkable of Rob Mimpriss's pieces there is a skill, and a mystery and elusiveness to that skill, which other short-story writers might envy. This is a masterful collection.'

Gee Williams

'heaving with loss, regret and familial bonds.'

Annexe Magazine

Printed in Great Britain
by Amazon

41780297R00096